RED AND HER DRAGONS

A REVERSE HAREM SHIFTER FAIRYTALE RETELLING

LISA CULLEN

OTHER TITLES BY LISA CULLEN

Lisa's books are steamy, standalone, shifter romances with an HEA and FREE to read in Kindle Unlimited.

Dirty Paranormal Fairytale Haremland Series (this series)

Beauty and Her Beasts | Alice and Her Shifters | Goldie and Her Bears | Red and Her Dragons | Cinderella and Her Vampires

Shifters of Beaver Brook Series

Diego | Landon | Aldo | Barrett | Darion

Lisa's Box Set Deals

Her Three Fated Mates

Shifter Protection

Six Shifters for Christmas

DESCRIPTION

Trouble brewed on the horizon. It was me. **I was trouble.**
My coven promised me to the wolves. But my fiancé was an abusive
jerk I couldn't get away from.
He had to be proven unfit. The only way I could do that was spy on
him when he left in the middle of the night.

What I heard lead me back to an ex-boyfriend.

Once I got a taste of what I was missing, I couldn't go back to the
wolves. Not anymore.
I was home again, with **my three hot as hell dragon shifters who
knew exactly how to get under my skin.**
But war was brewing. And all shifters were in danger. *Especially
my men.*

Well, little did this army know of who they were dealing with.
To get to my men, you have to deal with me first.
And I'm a lot more powerful than I look.

PROLOGUE: EMILY

Emily shot upright in bed, startled by the sudden silence and the dark. The house around her was unnaturally quiet. It was the sort of quiet that shocked her system. The sort of quiet that let her know Rowan, her fiancé, wasn't around.

His disappearing act had been happening a lot recently. She never knew where he took off too. Only that he wasn't where he should have been. Not that she really minded. Her engagement was an arrangement since before she was born. One that she hated.

Emily pulled herself from the bed and went to the kitchen to get a drink of water. On the way, she thought about how often he left in the middle of the night. It was almost every night now. And the only issue she had was not knowing when he was going to return.

The last beating he gave her for trying to leave was still evident in the form of bruises that covered her body in convenient to areas that wouldn't show outside her clothes. She hated living with the wolves. Most of all, she hated living with him in his small cabin.

Once she downed the small glass of water, she leaned against the counter and stared into the darkness that covered the little cabin while her thoughts took over.

If she could prove Rowan's infidelity and disloyalty to the agreement of her betrothal, she would be free and there wasn't a damn thing he could do to stop her. She knew she should stay where she was until she knew for sure, but she was tired of waiting on her chance to leave.

His disappearing act was turning out to be almost nightly. And she refused to stick around and watch her life roll by under Rowan's control. She would rather die than do any such thing.

Emily nodded to herself, convinced this time was the last, and moved to her room to pull on some clothes. She dressed as dark as she could, which was a pair of jeans, a black tank top, and a pair of boots.

She pulled her long red hair back into a low ponytail and slipped on a leather jacket before stepping out of the cabin and into the shadows. Though she didn't have a clue as to where he went off to at night, she figured if she searched long enough, she would find him.

It wasn't long until she found him deep in the woods. And though she had suspected he wasn't going to be alone, she never thought she would find him with his father, Bryson, the Alpha of the wolf pack. Even more surprising, there were four humans standing with them.

She carefully inched closer to get an idea of what they were talking about, shoving the large dose of disappointment that he wasn't with another woman as far down as she could push it. She really would have rather found him sleeping with someone than stumble upon a secret meeting, but at least she might learn why he was sneaking out so often.

Keeping herself to the shadows, and as quietly as she could, she settled next to a tree, close enough to hear most of what the group was saying, even though they were talking in hushed tones as to not let their voices carry through the night.

"You promised us he would be found by now," one of the humans said. He sounded as though he was accustomed to getting his way. He stood in front of the group of humans, pointing a finger at Bryson and Rowan.

Bryson sighed. "And we are searching for him."

"Not to mention the traps are expensive," Rowan added.

"We're tired of waiting on you," the same human said. "We're ready to take matters into our own hands if Kai isn't handed over soon."

"We had an agreement," Bryson spat back, taking a step closer to the human in charge. The three men standing behind their leader stepped closer, hands going to their sides. Likely firearms.

"One that will be forfeited if you don't hold up your end of the bargain," the human said.

Emily rolled everything over in her mind. The humans were hunting for someone named Kai. They hired the wolves to find this person, and the wolves were proving unsuccessful. Though she had no clue what they had offered the wolves to get them to work with humans, she suspected it was something Bryson desperately needed. The only thing she could figure was control. He thrived on it. What he could gain control over that he didn't already have was beyond her at the time. However, the hunt of this person was where Rowan went at night. That much was for certain.

Regardless, she realized the traps that had been causing unnecessary harm to the neighboring shifter colonies were because of the wolves, and that was enough to make her disgusted. But when the human mentioned Kai and that brought on a whole new level of urgency.

Though Emily didn't know the guy personally, she knew Marcus did. Kai was one of his friends.

The meeting sounded like it was close to being over, which prompted Emily to turn around and sneak off into the shadows. She needed to get to Marcus soon and warn him about Kai. If he didn't already know. Either way, this was her last shot at freedom.

As she moved, her foot rolled on a rock, sending her plummeting to the ground. She grabbed a branch to stop her fall but the thing broke off. The whole thing put off too much noise, alerting the group to her presence.

"Who's there?" Bryson called out.

Rowan shifted into his wolf, judging by the sound of the growl.

Emily didn't want to risk getting caught. She had no choice. She tried to run, but it was a wasted effort. Rowan tackled Emily to the ground. Bryson slowly stepped forward and put pressure on the ankle she rolled. Emily groaned, burying her face into the moist earth.

"You know the rules, witch," Bryson spat.

"As do you," Emily retorted.

Rowan shifted back to his human form and looked to his father for direction, like the obedient dog he was.

Bryson said, "Maybe a few days locked up will break her of this constant disobedience."

Rowan nodded. "Yes, Alpha."

Emily rolled her eyes. Not once could she recall him ever calling Bryson dad or father, or anything in between.

Rowan picked up Emily by her hair and dragged her back to the pack. He tossed her into her room and locked the door, barring it from the outside. She banged on it several times to no avail. Rowan was already gone.

Emily threw her back against the door and looked around her room for a way out. There had to be a way out. She had to get to Marcus, and she would be damned if one of his friends died because she got caught sneaking in on a secret meeting.

And if Rowan tried to stop her again, she would give him a taste of his own medicine.

* * *

Marcus

Marcus stood on his balcony, processing the discussion he just had with his two roommates. The meeting with Bret and Jax went about as well as expected.

Once they made it to the war room, each of them took their seat while he stood looking over the map of the region. After several seconds Bret said, "Don't keep us in suspense, my man. Tell us what's going on."

Marcus huffed. "Someone is hunting us."

"Do you know who?" Jax asked.

Marcus shook his head. "Whoever it is, I have a strong suspicion that shifters are working with them to help."

"Is this about the uptick in traps being laid out?" Bret asked.

Marcus nodded. "The situation has grown dire, and we need to get to the bottom of this, and last week."

"What do you need us to do?" Jax asked, rising to the occasion.

Marcus pointed at the map. "We need to cover a large amount of land, taking out all the traps we find and searching for the ones laying them too."

"We can take turns patrolling," Jax said. "I'll go first."

Marcus shook his head. "I'll do the first round. Then Bret. You take the last."

Jax nodded.

The plan was in place, but that didn't bring Marcus any comfort. He normally didn't spend much time on his balcony. It was Emily's favorite spot. But she was gone. Somehow, the spot still calmed him. He continued to process through the meeting and the plan when a voice echoed through the night air.

"Marcus!"

That voice, he thought. It was familiar but he couldn't place where or why.

And then it hit him.

Emily.

He searched the direction her voice had come from and once he caught sight of her, rushed to meet her. As he ran, he smelled blood on her. Fresh blood. That urged his feet to move faster. She slammed into his body and collapsed. He quickly took stock of her appearance.

She was pretty beaten up.

He scooped her into his arms and carried her back to the castle. Once he got her settled on the couch, he collected his first aid things and then returned to her.

"What happened?" he asked as he sat on his knees taking stock of her injuries.

"I snuck out to see if I could catch Rowan in something that would break the contract on our engagement," she said and then winced as Marcus cleaned her scrapped knuckles with an alcohol wipe.

"Sorry," he murmured. "Please continue."

She took in a breath. "What I found was a secret meeting between him, his father, and a group of humans. They are looking for Kai and setting expensive traps. Kai is your friend, right?"

Marcus met Emily's hazel gaze.

He never expected Emily would have the pieces of the puzzle he needed to solve. But he was never more grateful that she had. He cleared his throat. "Yes. I know him. Did they say what they wanted him for?"

She shook her head. "I didn't get that far. My guess is they had to have offered Bryson something he couldn't refuse to stoop low enough to work with humans. I can only think of a few things that would do that, and none of them are good."

Marcus nodded and continued to clean up Emily's battered body.

His worst fears were confirmed. And it was about to get worse.

"What happened to you?" he asked.

"I got caught and locked in my room. When I tried to escape, Rowan did what he does best…"

"He beat you?" Marcus said, trying hard to hide the anger that boiled through his veins.

She shrugged. "You should see how he came out of it."

Marcus smirked. "Bret taught you well."

"He did." She smiled and winced.

"Well, you're safe here," Marcus said. "And you're welcome to stay as long as you would like."

"Thank you," she said. "Because I'm never going back there."

"You can stay forever then," Marcus said with a smile.

"I couldn't put you out," she said. "But I'll stay here for a little while. Just until I get back on my feet, so to speak."

Marcus nodded and finished addressing Emily's wounds. He then took her to the guest room. The same room she used to have. Once she was inside, he gave her a set of clothes to change into and bade her a quick goodnight before leaving to go do his rounds. Now that he knew who the target was and most of who was behind the traps, he had an idea of what to look for. In the morning, he planned to stop by Chase's place to learn what he can from Kai. He would pass along the information to Bret and Jax once he got back.

1

EMILY

The second I opened my eyes, I stretched my arms above my head, ignoring the protest in my still sore body. Slowly, over the next few days, the soreness would fade. Especially with the way I slept. Last night was the best night's sleep I had in a long time. Years even.

I climbed out of bed and shuffled my way toward the kitchen, still wearing the oversized sweats and t-shirt Marcus lent me. My feet brushed along the marble floor as I moved. It wasn't long before the sounds of breakfast being made in the kitchen reached me. Soon after, I listened to the way Jax and Bret were giving each other hell. My lips stretch wider in response.

It had been a little over two years since I was in this castle. And that's what the place was. Almost cliché considering dragon shifters lived here, but it was home. The castle had always been a home to me. This was my safe place.

Before I rounded the corner that led into the kitchen, I stopped and poked my head into the room. Bret and Jax stood with their backs toward me. Another smile stretched my lips as a plan formulated in my mind. Though it was never a great idea to sneak up on dragons, much less these two, I couldn't help myself. I really wanted to surprise them.

Of course, that also meant banking on the hope Marcus hadn't told them I was back yet.

I bit my bottom lip and silently stepped into the room. Once I made it to the island, I quietly pulled out a chair and took a seat. A few seconds later, I said, "Good morning, boys."

Both Bret and Jax turned around and set their shock-filled eyes on me. They smiled and shouted my name. Both men rushed me, pulling me from the chair, and then took turns swooping me into their arms and squeezing me close.

I laughed as I pulled away. "I'm happy to see you too."

"I hope you're hungry," Bret said. His blond hair was cut military short, though a thick layer of fuzz covered the bottom half of his face. His silver eyes took in mine. He stood a whole head taller than me and was covered in thick, hard muscle.

"I could eat," I said and scratched at his beard. "What's this?"

He chuckled. "I like to call it a beard."

"Is that what they are calling those things these days?" I asked.

"I've been slaving away all morning on this feast," Jax said, returning to his spot in front of the stove. He was jovial considering the normally serious moods I have known him to have. His dark brown hair was pulled back in a low ponytail that rested against the nape of his neck. He turned his attention toward me as he picked up the spatula, settling his ice-blue eyes on mine. "So, you better be hungry."

"I am starving," I said as I retook my seat at the island in the center of the kitchen. "So, how have you guys been?"

Bret shrugged. "Eh, now that you're here, I'm certainly doing better. But things haven't been too bad for me."

"Same," Jax said.

"A man of so many words," I commented. "Glad to see that hasn't changed."

"You know me so well," he said and then flipped an egg.

"Where's Marcus?" I asked, looking around for him.

"On patrol," Jax said. "He'll be back in a few hours."

"The man is all work and no play," Bret said. "Which is fine by me. His loss is my gain."

He winked, forcing my cheeks to set on fire. I cleared my throat as a plate was placed in front of me, piled high with bacon, scrambled eggs, sausage links, hash brown patties, and a bowl of blueberries.

"Wow, this is too much," I said.

"Don't worry," Jax said, pointing his spatula at Bret. "Whatever you don't eat, Mr. Hoover here would suck it up for you."

I laughed and dug in. My stomach growled in anticipation. I wrapped an arm around my torso to help smother the sound.

Bret snorted. "You're the bottomless pit here."

"True," Jax agreed. He patted his belly

Minutes later, Bret was handed a plate. He took a seat on my right. A few more minutes longer, and Jax had a plate and sat down at my left. Each of them smiled and I suddenly became self-conscious about how I ate. But the food was too delicious. With each bite, I cared less and less.

The food was five stars compared to the slop and scraps I would get with the wolves. And that was only when I was fed. There were times where, just for punishment, I would be deprived. Never for longer for a day, and it wasn't like I had minded either. Their food lacked sustenance, flavor, and probably nutrition.

I wondered if that was why they were always angry.

A few minutes into the meal, Bret and Jax started in with the questions I knew I was going to have to face, sooner or later.

"It's so good to see you again," Jax said. "But I can't help but wonder why you left in the first place?"

"Yeah," Bret said. "I mean, I never saw you as an arranged marriage type of girl."

"Well, there is no longer a marriage to arrange," I said. "Besides, it was what my family wanted. I had no say in the matter."

"What changed?" Jax asked.

"Well..." I started.

The men slid in closer, and I breathed in deep their musky, woodsy scents, instantly becoming aroused. I sucked in a breath of shock with how incredibly hot and bothered I became. Though I knew these men for a long time, I had always only thought of them as nothing more than big brothers. But there was something different about them now. Clearly, they were much, much more than that to my raging, neglected hormones.

The sensation was something that I knew was going to be almost impossible to ignore.

But before I could let myself get too carried away, I put my full attention into my food and pushed my dirty thoughts to the side.

For the moment.

"You mean you didn't want to marry some random guy you've never met before?" Bret asked.

I laughed. "It's every girl's fantasy. I thought you knew that."

"I skipped that day in school," he said. "What changed?"

I shrugged, unwilling to answer the question. All the while, I had to face the music at some point.

"Did he at least treat you right?" Jax said with a dangerous tone in his voice.

I snorted. "You clearly have never met him or his father."

Jax's eyes turned shades darker, deepening into a deep ocean blue. Bret's darkened from soft grey to a deep stone color, almost the shade of storm clouds.

I gulped. Since when did they become so overprotective over me?

"I'm going to kill him," Jax said.

"Not before I get to him first," Bret said. "Death would be a kindness to him. That's something I'm going to make sure he doesn't get until I'm done with him."

"Hey, I'm not exactly weak, you know," I said, taking some unnecessary offense to their chivalry. "Besides, I handled everything already."

"What happened?" Jax asked. He enunciated each word.

"Explain 'handled everything,'" Bret said.

I took in a deep breath and held up my hands. "Okay, okay. You both are going to need to sit back and give a lady some room to breathe."

They did so and I took in another breath as I decided on where to start. "I'll start from the beginning…"

By the time I was done, my half-eaten breakfast had grown cold and forgotten about. When I got to the parts about having had enough and gave Rowan a taste of his own medicine, the men cheered for me.

I laughed. Oh, how I had missed them.

"So, long story short, that was not only what happened, but what I meant by 'handled everything.'"

"I'm proud of you," Bret said, clapping me on the shoulder and giving it a firm squeeze.

"Well, your lessons have paid off," I said.

"That's my girl," Jax said.

"She's not a girl anymore," Bret said. "She's grown into one hell of a powerful woman."

I blushed. "It's only been a few years since we saw each other last… hardly long enough to grow up. Not in the way you implied anyway."

"Be that as it may," Jax said. "You have changed. And though I hate the thought of that man putting his hands on you, I'm glad he wasn't able to break your spirit."

"More importantly, the change was for the better," Bret added with a wink.

"Stop it, you too… Sheesh," I said, playing off the effect their compliments had on me.

"Well, if you need anything," Jax said, standing from the island and collecting the plates, "let us know."

"Since you mentioned it," I said. "I noticed the system in the living room when I got here last night. Anyone want to play a video game?"

Both men smiled.

"Absolutely," Jax said.

"I have to leave soon, unfortunately," Bret said.

"Well that sucks," I said and pouted.

"Hold on now…" Bret held up a hand, grinning from ear to ear. "I was going to say I would love to join for as long as I can."

I stood from the island and headed to the living room. "I'll get everything set up."

A video game was exactly what I needed to keep my mind off having sex with the men. And it worked. Right up to the point where we stood to see Bret off for his patrol.

We walked him to the door, he turned around and winked again. "Don't have too much fun while I'm gone."

I laughed. "Don't be too jealous, I have zero plans for the day."

"I'll keep her busy," Jax said.

"I stand by what I said," Bret said, glaring at Jax. "Take care of her."

"Oh, I plan to," he said, shoving Bret off the doorstep. "Now go uphold your solemn duty."

I rolled my eyes, even though my lips had failed to stop smiling one slightest bit.

Bret shook his head. "Careful Jax, you know what happened the last time."

"Yeah, yeah, yeah..." Jax waved him off.

Bret smirked, setting his gaze on me as he turned and shifted into his dragon. Black scales rippled over his frame as he stretched and grew. His wings unfurled and he flapped them once before launching off the ground, taking flight. I never got used to watching the men shift. But I also never stopped finding myself in awe at the massive creature before me.

Beautiful and magnificent.

Once he left, Jax turned and faced me. He smiled at me, gazing into my eyes from under his dark lashes. "Now you're all mine."

I laughed off the comment, but his words made my heart skip a beat.

He threw his arm over my shoulder and walked with me back to the couch, squeezing me closer to him. It was going to be hard to keep my hands off him.

"Now about that rematch..." he let his words trail off.

I chuckled. "You're so on."

2

MARCUS

After finishing my patrol shift, I decided to pay a visit to Kai. He needed to know that the traps were set for him, and I needed to figure out why. The sooner I could get to the bottom of what was going on, the sooner I could put a stop to it.

I landed closer to the cabin than I normally would have. But time was of the essence, and as soon as I got the information I needed, I could return to the castle and share the news with Bret and Jax.

Before approaching the door, I took a closer look around the area for signs of traps. The last thing I wanted was to get a call that one of them had been seriously hurt or killed by one of them because I didn't spend the time making sure their property was clear.

After an hour of looking, and finding nothing, I figured the hunters hadn't come out this far just yet. But it was only a matter of time before they did. Until that time came to pass, I needed to get information to fill in the blanks of what I already knew.

I continued toward the cabin.

Once I arrived at the door, I barely had the chance to knock before it was opened. Cassie stood in the opened doorway. She smiled at me.

"Good morning, Cassie," I said.

"Hey, Doc!" she said. "I saw you coming toward the front door. What brings you by?"

I nodded. "I needed to speak with Kai. Is he around?"

"He is almost always here. Come on in," she said and pushed the screen door open to allow me through.

I stepped in and was astonished by all the changes Cassie had made to the place. I raked my gaze over the front room just admiring everything. The windows were free of dirt and dust, and allowed in the light from the outside which created a nice warmth to the space. The floorboards shone with fresh wax. All the dust that had coated everything was cleared. Even from in the corners of the ceiling. There was a strange scent that filled the air as well. What it was escaped my recollection, and I didn't bother with trying to figure it out. I had other more pressing matters to address.

"Well, this place looks very different," I said. "You definitely had a positive effect on things here."

"Thank you. The place needed a more feminine touch, don't you think?" she said.

I nodded. "It's quite an improvement."

"Make yourself at home," Cassie said, gesturing toward the couch. "I'll go let Kai know you're here."

Cassie took off down the hall that led to the bathroom and two bedrooms. I took another gander around the place as I took a seat on the couch. Even the fireplace was free from soot. And scrubbed clean to the point I could pick out each individual brick and where it's mortar laid.

"Who's here?" Chase called from the kitchen.

"It's only me, Chase," I said and twisted toward the kitchen.

Chase poked his head around the corner.

I nodded, meeting his gaze.

"Oh. Hey Marcus," he said. "What brings you by?"

"I had some information for Kai," I said.

Jasper stepped out of the hall and into the living room. "Marcus, what a nice surprise."

"I'm afraid I'm not here for good reasons," I said.

"Oh?" he asked, continuing to move into the living room he took a seat on the opposite end of the couch. "What's up?"

"I have news regarding the traps," I said. "Specifically, news for Kai."

Jasper nodded and leaned against the back of the couch and crossed his arms over his chest. Cassie came back in and joined his side.

"He's on his way," she said.

"Thank you," I said and nodded once. Seconds later, Kai entered the room, pulling down his t-shirt over the waistband of his jeans before running his hands through his hair as he made his way to the seat next to me.

"Hey Marcus," he said. "You needed me?"

I nodded. "I have information about the traps. Particularly news involving you."

"I'm listening," he said. His eyes stared at me, filled with caution. His lips curved downward.

"You may want to take a seat," I suggested.

He shook his head. "I'm fine. Tell me."

"They were placed for you," I said. "You wouldn't happen to be able to tell me why that is, would you?"

Kai took a seat as his lungs deflated. He leaned forward, lowering his head to his chest. He huffed as he propped himself up on his knees. A few moments later, he nodded. In a low, barely audible voice he said, "I killed someone."

I sucked in a breath and arched an eyebrow. "Who?"

"I would like to know when," Chase said.

He shook his head as he continued to stare at the floor. "She was my girlfriend. I thought I was in love. She knew what I was and wanted me to change her. I was willing to do that, but... one night, I was angry. Too angry. I lost control over my bear and shifted. She was too close. And I was too late."

"That's what you meant by deadly consequences?" Cassie asked, her voice somber.

He nodded. "I'll understand if this changes things between us. And ever since that night, I distanced myself from everyone. Until Cassie came along."

Chase added. "And that was a struggle trying to convince him she wasn't an evil witch who was after everything."

"Hell, getting him to accept the two of us was like pulling teeth," Jasper said.

I nodded as I listened, taking everything in.

"Yeah, no kidding. We barely wiggled our way into his life, and not without a fight or two on top of it," Chase said.

"Where is the family now?" I asked Kai.

"On the other side. I had to put as much distance between me and them as I could get. There was no way I could bring their daughter back, and though I was willing to lay down my life to make up for hers, death would have been merciful," Kai said.

I nodded. "They must have followed you here."

"Years later," Kai muttered. "But I didn't make it a secret about where I was."

"Why didn't you stay there and accept responsibility for your actions?" I asked.

"To what end?" Kai asked. "It didn't seem to make a difference. I couldn't bring her back. Besides, they understood it was an accident. I banished myself to save them the grief of constantly seeing me, and I had set out to live the rest of my life in solitude and exile. The last thing I want is for someone else to get hurt because of me."

"How long ago was this?" Chase asked again.

"I was sixteen," Kai said.

I gasped. "You were new. It's no wonder the parents accepted banishment as punishment."

"But why now?" Cassie asked.

"Why now, what?" I asked.

"Why come after him now? If it's been years, then why bother with looking for him now?" she asked.

I shrugged. "That is what I'm trying to figure out. Hopefully, I can find the answer before a war breaks out. And let me be clear, I'm not saying they are the ones responsible for this hunt. I still have that to figure out."

"People on the other side don't forget, much less forgive easily. I suspect they want some closure or retribution for their daughter's death, even though I had explained everything to them," Kai said.

"They must have changed their mind because they are willing to start a war to get you," Jasper said.

"Stopping by their place would be the next step in my plan, but I'll likely send Bret to do that. He's the only one that could pull off being a private investigator," I said.

"I wish I could help, but I don't even know where they live anymore," Kai said. "I let that life behind me fade away."

"I'll see what I can do," I said. "Meanwhile, I strongly suggest you don't leave this cabin until things blow over. Whoever is behind this is also working with the wolves."

"You're kidding," Jasper said.

"I wouldn't joke about anything like this, but no, I'm not," I said.

"What do you suggest we do?" Chase said.

I paused to think things over. There was only one thing to do. Keep Kai alive for as long as possible. That meant keeping him out of harm's way, which also meant, out of sight.

"Keep Kai here. I'll come back with more information as I come across it. If you see anything or notice anyone lurking around who shouldn't be, call me. I'll be here as soon as I can. With some luck, we can put a stop to this before anyone else gets hurt," I said.

"I'll do what I can as well," Cassie offered. "Even if that's just entertaining Kai, so he doesn't go crazy."

"You will?" Kai asked. Shock filled his voice.

She smiled. "Don't be ridiculous. Of course, I would."

Kai smirked. "Thank you."

"You're welcome," she said.

Things fell silent. I took that as my signal to leave.

"I should get going," I said.

"Thank you," Kai said and stood from the couch. "And I'm sorry for how my actions have impacted others.

I stood and said, "I have a feeling this is more than just you. But the only information I had got had mentioned you. Don't let it tear you up. Stay out of sight and let me know if anything changes."

Once I stepped outside, I raked my gaze over every shadow within the woods surrounding the cabin and then at the sky. I had a bad feeling about what was to come, and I had a sinking suspicion things were going to escalate sooner rather than later.

3

EMILY

Gaming with Jax was fun. I had missed how easy it was to be around him and Bret and Marcus. I almost forgot that being around them was almost easier than breathing. Being back felt amazing. Better than I ever hoped.

By the time lunch rolled around, I was ready to work out. It had been a while, and I was anxious to get back into the routine. Rowan hated the idea that I was physically strong and had forbidden me from doing anything that would threaten his fragile masculinity. And for the sake of my family and whatever they were getting in the arrangement they had made since before the time I was born, I was forced to comply.

Mostly.

I did what I could not to lose too much of what I had learned. Pushups against the counter, wall sits, sit-ups... things like that. I refused to leave everything I was behind me. But now that I was in the place I had always wanted to be, I realized just how much of myself I had lost after all.

Still... I had to find a way out of the game Jax and I were playing, so I let one of the non-playable characters kill me with its plasma sword.

Jax cried out in playful defeat. "No! I shall avenge you!"

I laughed. "I think I'm better off dead. Besides I'm ready to move on to something else."

"Lunch?" he asked.

"Not yet," I said, shaking my head.

He reached for the controller. I handed it to him, and he placed both on the coffee table in front of him after he turned off the machine. He leaned back against the couch and smiled at me.

I giggled and settled my attention on the controllers resting on the coffee table. I couldn't allow myself to fall too far into the moment. It was likely only going to be short-lived.

"So," Jax said, playfully poking me in my side. "What do you want to do next with your newly found freedom."

My eyes met his icy blues. It was so hard not to fall into them. My arousal hiked. I had to get my hormones under control. In the past, what helped me was rigorous exercise, followed by a cold shower. There was only one thing I figured could meet that expectation. My lips stretched over my teeth. "Sparring."

He smiled in that boyish way he normally flashed at me, but this time, I was completely dazzled by it. He fist-bumped the air. "Yeah! Now, we're talking."

I giggled, but I had to force the heat from my face. I couldn't let it slip what he did to me. Knowing him, he would tease me to no end. It was better that I kept this new development to myself for as long as possible. I stood from the couch, faced him, and said, "Lead the way."

"You forgot how to get there?" he asked, jokingly. "You've been away for far too long."

"Just stand up and go, would you?" I asked, adding a little more force to my words but keeping things playful still.

He let out an exaggerated sigh and took his time standing. Once his feet were fully planted on the marble floor, he snapped his finger and pointed in the direction of where we were going. "Follow me."

"Thank you," I said. "Was that so hard?"

He peeked over his shoulder at me. There was a glint of something in his eyes that hiked up my heart rate. He didn't say anything. His look said enough. I sucked in a breath and forced more of my recently out-of-control hormones deep down.

"We're following the leader, the leader, the leader," he sang.

I laughed again and fell into step behind him as he led the way from the living room to the training room in the basement. As he moved, I couldn't help my eyes falling to his ass, wrapped in his tight jeans, moving from side to side.

I bit my lip and thought to myself how much I needed this little workout…especially the cold shower afterward.

We made it to the training room in a blink of an eye and I instantly walked to the center of the mat.

Jax's eyes glinted in delight as I took my ready stance and waited for him to join me. "Careful, darling… you very well might get more than you bargained for."

"We'll see. Now shut up and spar with me," I said.

"With pleasure," he murmured and took his stance in front of me.

"No powers… and no cheating," I said.

"You're no fun." He smirked.

I chuckled. "I'm still human."

"I can see that," he said, letting his eyes drift along my length before returning to my gaze. He sighed wistfully, hamming up the whole desire of using his powers. Though he didn't normally cheat when it came to sparring—if memory served right—he did love to use his powers. Besides, cheating was more Bret's forte. "Very well. No powers."

I nodded and then tried to kick his side, which he expertly blocked.

"Nice try, kitten, but you'll have to do better than that," he said. There was a hint of seriousness to him, which reminded me of the good old days.

I glared at him, took a step closer, and threw a right hook. Jax grabbed my arm and tucked it under his then planted a palm strike into my chest. Thankfully he barely hit me. A strike like that, with enough force, could stop a beating heart. But it told me one valuable thing.

I was severely out of practice.

But I wasn't about to let him get the upper hand. I went to kick out his knee, which he blocked, and then swept my feet out from underneath me. I landed on my back on the matt with him on top of me in an arm lock. When he placed pressure, I patted the mat. He released my arm, and we took our stances again.

"Not bad," he said. "A little rusty, but not bad."

I quirked an eyebrow. "A little rusty?"

He shrugged as he took his stance again. "I don't blame you. It was simply an observation."

I smirked. "You've gotten slower, old man."

He wasn't an old man. Quite the opposite. He was probably only five or six years older than me if memory served me correctly. But I knew what he was trying to do, and I was giving him a taste of his own brutal honesty.

"Slow, you say?" he asked. "Maybe I was simply trying to take things at your pace."

I took my stance, holding my fists in front of my face. "Prove it."

As he took his stance, the air pulled toward him, surrounding him in a bubble of wind. His feet left the floor as the pull of the wind whipped at my hair. I glared at him.

"I said no powers." My voice barely carried through the rush of air filling the room.

He winked. "You told me to prove it."

"Yeah, but not with your powers. I'm still squishy. Remember?" Though it felt like I was screaming, my voice barely came out louder than a whisper.

He still heard me though.

I knew that because he frowned at me as he started to lower to the ground. The wind around us died. The second his feet were on the floor again, he approached me.

"You do realize you have powers too, right?"

I nodded. "None that I'm willing to use on you. Even in practice. You should already know why."

He nodded. "Well, I guess I'll have to show you this way then."

Before I had the chance to blink, my back was pinned to his chest. His left arm pinned my upper chest to him. His right arm had slid under mine and around the back of my head. I was in his personal brand of a chokehold. And there was no escape.

My breath left my lungs.

Jax brought his lips closer to my ear. His breath poured over my skin in warm waves, creating sensations I had been desperately trying to fight off as he said, "What was that about being slow again?"

Goosebumps prickled along my skin. I sucked in a deep breath and smirked, even though he couldn't see it. I then slipped my fingers between his arm and my chest and pressed on the pressure point as I stomped on his foot.

Both actions caused him to release me. I rolled away from him, ending upright on my feet, and pivoted to face him in my ready stance.

"Clever," he said. "I'm impressed."

My stomach growled embarrassingly loud.

"And you're hungry." He ran his fingers through his long dark brown hair. "How about lunch?"

I shrugged. "I could eat."

He chuckled. "You barely ate breakfast, and your stomach is saying otherwise."

"How so?" I asked and stepped out of my stance.

"You're starving. Let's take care of that." He started to turn around but stopped halfway. "BLTs sound all right?"

"You had me at B," I said. "But I really need to shower first."

"Why?"

"Because we just got done sparring. I'm sweaty, and body odor and bacon don't necessarily mix well."

He laughed. "Shower after. Eat first."

He turned and walked away, leaving little room for argument.

"Fine, but I want to spar more after we eat," I said.

He laughed as he continued to walk away. "One beating isn't enough for you?"

I shrugged, even though he couldn't see it. "You hardly beat me."

"Sounds like you need another demonstration." He turned to face me. I stopped, staring at him in confusion.

He used his index finger pointing to the ground, swirling it in a circle.

"What happened to food?" I asked.

He chuckled. "This won't take long."

I sighed and turned around, heading back into the training room. Now I had two sensations to contend with. Hunger and arousal.

It was an interesting mix, but I really didn't mind. This time with Jax was exactly what I needed.

4

JAX

I had missed Emily in ways I couldn't describe. We all did. Me, Marcus, and Bret.

She made a change in all of us when she came into our lives. Marcus had met her first. Dated her for the longest time. Right up to the day when she left us to go live with the wolves. She was so smooth and easy to be around. She made everything easier.

But she found out about what her family had done, and that messed with her a lot. After waiting for her to leave on her own, they came to us and nearly knocked our door down to get her.

Our choices were to either let her go or start a war with the local coven and wolf pack.

Of course, she left. She had no other options. Though it was diffi-cult to let her go back then, I had a feeling she was going to be back.

And I was right. She came back, and I was more than happy to get in all the time I could with her.

She was quite the firecracker. Though it was hard to believe, she had grown more beautiful with her absence. It was hard to ignore the sensations that rushed through my blood when she was near me. And I could smell her arousal on her, which made it all the more difficult to keep my hands off of her.

But if anyone was going to take her though, it needed to be Marcus. He deserved as much respect. She was his before she was even on my radar. But the tiny fact didn't mean the struggle wasn't real. It would be easy to take her. I could make her melt into the palm of my hand.

A little kiss on the cheek... a soft touch on her skin... and she would be as good as mine.

But I owed Marcus my life, and I knew how he felt about her. As much as I wanted her, I had to wait. I needed to give him the chance to rekindle things with her. It would feel too much like a cheap move to swoop in and steal her right from under his nose.

Sparring with her was the most fun I had in a long while, though it made it slightly more difficult to ignore her arousal, driving me and my dragon a little bit crazy. She had some real skills and talent. And the way she wrapped her legs around me... I was rather surprised that she hadn't lost much of her training while she was with the dogs of Washington.

But she wasn't the only one that had changed. I was changing too. All because of her. I wasn't much of a jokester. That was Bret's department. But with Emily, it was easy to find things to tease her about.

"What was that move?" I asked.

She tried to do a roundhouse kick, but it was sloppy and lacked the uniformity it needed to really land right. In her defense, she had been laughing the entire time, which only added to the hilarity of what I saw.

"What do you mean?" she asked, playing dumb.

I imitated her move and threw in a little spice for flavor. She laughed. I loved hearing her laugh. That sound was exactly what this place was missing.

"Making fun of me now, are you?" she asked. "That's a low blow."

I shrugged. "You're the one giving me plenty of ammunition to use against you. But it's understandable. You're a bit out of practice."

She propped her hands on her round hips and glared at me. Her thick red hair spilled around her shoulders. Sweat made some of the strands stick to her forehead and cheeks. The whole image was sexy.

Hot as hell. I once again struggled against the urge to take her again. The only thing stopping me was my respect for Marcus and how much I valued our friendship. And he was more than a friend to me. He was my brother. "I'm better on the ground anyway. But I'll get there."

"Why didn't you keep up on your forms?" I asked.

She dropped her arms to her sides and sighed. "I'll give you three guesses and the first two don't count."

I nodded. "Fair enough. Though the guy is making me like him less and less and I didn't have much love for him to begin with."

"You and me, both," she said. "I didn't exactly have room or freedom to do much of anything but punch my mattress and even then, that rarely happened. I suspect most of what I still have is just muscle memory."

"Possibly." I smirked and then asked, "So, you're better on the ground, you say?"

She giggled and glanced up at me from under her lashes. Her woodsy brown eyes held mine for a moment before falling to her plump lips. I held my breath for fear I would lose my control and throw out all my better judgment in favor of seeing what they tasted like.

I cleared my throat. "Well?"

She got down on the floor. "Don't say I didn't warn you."

Everything in me was screaming that this was a bad idea. But I couldn't resist her. She laid on the ground with her legs bent and spread wide. I instantly thought of her naked, pussy swollen and wet, practically begging for my dick to fill her.

The position sent my mind into a frenzy.

"Scared?" she asked.

That sobered me, but only a little. I cleared my throat. "Hell no."

"Then what are you waiting for?" she asked.

I smirked and lowered myself to my knees at her side, bracing my upper body on my arms planted on either side of her.

She smiled. "You asked for this, just remember that."

I chuckled. "If you say so."

She reached up toward me. I instantly reacted, placing my knee on her belly and on hand on her hip, keeping her down. I met her smiling gaze for a moment. Within seconds, she managed to get me to my back, placing her knee on the inside of my right arm, her knee on my stomach, and her hand on my hip, holding me down.

I was, for the lack of a better phrase, surprisingly impressed.

"Well, would you look at that?" I said, smirking up at her.

She giggled. "I told you. Don't underestimate me."

"Consider my lesson learned," I said. "Though I wouldn't call this sparring."

"Is that so?" she asked.

I shook my head. "This is more like a playful wrestling match. I don't normally have this much fun with everyone."

She laughed. Her guard was dropped. I escaped her hold and placed her into one of my own. She laughed even harder.

"See? Playful wrestling match." I stared into her beautiful eyes, and my breath was stolen away from me. I wanted this to last forever. But I knew that wasn't a realistic expectation.

She nodded. "Okay, okay. You win. Let me up."

"First, answer me a question," I said, putting a little more pressure on her to keep her down.

She settled her gaze on me, waiting expectantly. "Okay…"

"How long are you going to stay this time?" I asked.

"That's your burning question?" she asked me and then bucked me off her. I landed in a roll.

"Yes, that is my burning question," I said as I sat up and faced her.

She shrugged. "I don't know. I'm still undecided."

I pinned her down again and lowered my mouth to her ear to whisper, "Stay forever."

When I leaned up, she was still smiling. But she pulled her gaze away from me. A small crease appeared in between her eyebrows. The image was confusing. I thought we were having a good time together.

"You have a beautiful smile," I said, pulling strands of deep red hair from in front of her face. "Never let it fade. For no one."

She shook her head and pushed me off of her, standing from the ground. "I need to go shower."

She turned and walked away. I followed her with my gaze until she turned out of sight. All the while, I was consumed with the struggle of not running after her to kiss her. It seemed like there was going to be a constant tug-of-war within me. So long as she was here, and Marcus hadn't patched things over with her, the battle between what I want and what I should probably do would continue.

With a sigh, I stood from the ground and continued to take deep breaths. My erection was refusing to go away. I throbbed with aching need, and Emily was the only thing who I knew would suffice. Since she was off-limits still, I decided maybe a cold shower was what I needed to do as well and went to do just that.

But halfway to my room, I had a change of mind.

5

EMILY

Jax followed me halfway to my room. "What about lunch?"

I continued walking and shook my head. "I need to shower first."

He grabbed my arm, forcing me to stop and face him. His dark hair was slick with sweat which made his ice blue eyes stand out even more. But instead of being playful, they were serious.

Welcome back, Jax.

"You need to eat," he said. "I could hear your stomach from the stairway."

I smiled. "I really need to shower. I stink."

He sniffed. "No. You don't."

"I would feel better showering first," I argued.

"Come on. Ten minutes is all I'm asking. That's long enough for you to eat a sandwich. Then you can take your shower," he added.

I stood silently considering his words. He had a point. It might be easier to work through all the hormones raging through my body if I had something on my stomach. Maybe good food would be a suitable substitute for what it really wants.

"I won't take no for an answer," Jax said and started pulling me toward the kitchen.

"I was actually going to agree with you," I muttered as he

continued to drag me along. "I can also walk for myself. I don't need you dragging me behind you."

"Fair enough." He released my arm and I fell into step behind him. "But just so you know, I wasn't going to drag you for very far. I was going to carry you."

"Yeah right," I muttered.

He turned around and leveled his serious gaze on me. "You don't believe I would?"

My heart skipped a beat. "No, I believe that you think you would. My willingness to be captured and carried is a whole other story."

He smirked as he listened. "All right then."

We continued toward the kitchen in silence for several moments. Then Jax spoke again.

"Do you usually need to consult with your conscience before making decisions?"

When it came to him and the other two men, apparently, I did. But I wasn't going to tell him that. "Not really. Was just weighing my options."

"And?" he asked as we stepped into the kitchen. He promptly went toward a cabinet next to the fridge and pulled out some bread before grabbing out some tomatoes, mayo, lettuce, and grated parmesan from the fridge.

"And I figured you may be right. I can't think on an empty stomach and though I desperately need that shower, having lunch first isn't going to be the end of the world. I can eat, and then I can get clean."

He chuckled to himself as he slapped a layer of mayo onto two slices of bread. He stacked slices of tomato on top of each with a leaf of lettuce before heading to the counter where the bacon sat leftover from breakfast. He swiped a few slices for each sandwich and then topped both off with another piece of bread. He handed one to me and took a seat at the island.

"So, why didn't you leave before now?" he asked around his bite.

I took the time to chew my first chunk of the sandwich before answering. Once I had swallowed it down, I shrugged. "As I said before, I needed proof to be let out of the arrangement. Otherwise, I would just be dragged right on back."

"You still could have come here," he said.

I met his gaze for a moment, and I wasn't sure what was behind his eyes but there was a seriousness in them again, which only added to my confusion. He was gorgeous and cryptic, and my hormones spiked again. Heat filled my neck, inching into my cheeks.

"I didn't think this place was an option," I said after swallowing down the last bite of food. "After how I left, I figured you three would want nothing else to do with me."

"You expected us to hate you for doing what your family needed you to do?" he asked, his eyebrows knitting themselves together.

I shrugged. "Yeah."

"Em... we could never hate you." His voice was soft. My heart skipped a beat.

His words hung in the air. My vision fell out of focus and something warm filled my hand. It pulled on my attention until I settled my gaze on his hand resting on mine. He stood from the island, pulling me into his hardened frame. His arms squeezed me into him.

"Never, ever think you are not welcomed here." He kissed the top of my head. "This is your home too. You'll always be home here."

I pulled away and tucked a strand of red hair behind my ear. This was an unexpected development, and I wasn't sure how to take it.

Jax lifted my chin with the tips of his fingers, forcing me to look him in the eyes. "Don't you ever forget that."

I nodded.

He lowered his mouth to mine, brushing my lips with his and creating a rush of heat and desire to flood through my system. He deepened the kiss, sliding his tongue into my mouth. I clung to him, kissing him back.

At the very precipice of my limits of holding back, Jax pulled away.

"Well?" he asked.

"I think I'm going to go take that shower now," I said and rushed out of the room.

I didn't stop until I reached the bathroom where I promptly turned on the shower and set it as cold as I could get. Once I was undressed, I climbed in.

My system was shocked by the cold, and I gasped at the iciness of the water as it poured unapologetically over my body. I braced myself against the wall of the shower and struggled to control my breathing.

But my hormones wouldn't fade completely.

My interaction with Jax was a close call. Too close. I had to come up with a better way of managing my desire for the men or I could be held responsible for breaking the arrangement. That was if it wasn't already broken. I hoped it was, but that didn't mean I should give in to my wonton desires.

Ten minutes later, I've had all I could take of the cold water and turned the shower setting to a much more comfortable, warmer temperature. All the while my mind processed through whether or not I really cared if I broke the agreement. I essentially did so anyway by leaving the way I did.

What did it matter if I had sex with the men I had grown to love very dearly over the years? Did I care about the fallout breaking the arrangement?

Probably not.

Still… I realized it was best to play everything on the safe side for now. And that meant finding another way to soothe the ache that had settled between my legs and refused to go away.

Though it wasn't exactly my first choice, I decided to use my hand. But not before my body was warmed up first.

I slid my fingers between my delicate folds and into the wetness of my sex. With my eyes closed, and the water beating down on my back, I rubbed my fingers along my clit in small circles, keeping a steady rhythm.

My orgasm started to build, and I concentrated on taking my time because I wanted this to be something that would help keep my hormones at bay for at least the rest of the day. Rushing was only going to cheapen the release. God knew I needed it.

I sighed as I continued to move my fingers in slow circles, resisting the rush of pleasure that built between my legs.

I thought about Jax. I thought about Bret. I thought about how they instantly set my nerves on fire. I thought about the way Jax's lips felt on mine. How his mouth tasted, and how my body nearly combusted. I even thought about the way it felt to have his arms wrapped around me.

Pressure increased. My breaths quickened. Warmth bled through me, mixing with the heat of the water splashing my skin. My movements quickened and I sucked in a breath as my orgasm hit.

I softly sighed through the waves of pleasure I pushed myself through. Once the orgasm faded, the water had started to turn cold again. That was my cue. With a still sexually frustrated sigh, I turned off the shower, climbed out, and dried off as I made my way back to my bed.

I collapsed on the bed and stared at the marble ceiling comparing the differences between the castle and the cabins of the wolf pack. The way the men responded to me was different as well.

Of all the memories I had of this place, I never thought I missed it as much as I had. Being back brought all those memories to the forefront of my mind. Here, I felt safe. Welcomed. Loved. Not to mentioned wanted.

With the wolves, and Rowan specifically, I felt shunned. Cast aside like yesterday's trash, and I was treated as though I wasn't a person.

Though I never understood why my family agreed to the arrangement, it wasn't unheard of for shifters to mix blood with witches. There was an old and unfounded belief that a witch's power somehow gave the children of the coupling powers. Though I had yet to meet a shifter with powers like a witch, there have been shifters born of a witch who ended up stronger in some way. Regardless, I considered myself lucky. A life bound to that horrible man was a life I wanted nothing to do with.

I was home. And there wasn't another place in this world or the next that I had ever felt as safe as I was here in the castle.

Seeing a different side to Bret and Jax was nice as well. Or maybe that was just me. Maybe I've become more receptive and observant.

Perhaps they were respecting Marcus enough to not try to pursue me. Now that we aren't in a relationship, perhaps I'm fair game.

Regardless, I would rather be chased by three gorgeous dragon shifters than one wolf.

But it would only be a matter of time before Rowan came to the castle. He would likely try to knock down the gates to get me back, maybe even start a war. If he was smart—him and his pathetic excuse of a father—they would stay far away from this place and give up on me.

I needed to let my family know before the wolves got to them. Surely, they would understand the arrangement was wrong for me.

I stood up to get dressed as my thoughts continued to rush through my mind. Despite everything, I missed being back. Things were just a little different now.

6

BRET

My shift was a long one filled with a whole lot of nothing but staring at trees. There was no sign of anything out of the ordinary, and I wondered how that was even possible. Marcus normally wasn't one to overstate the facts. If he said someone was laying traps for us, then I believed him. Still, if anyone was hiding within the trees, I didn't see them.

But now it was late in the afternoon, and my patrol was almost over. There was a part of me that was disappointed. Honestly, I wasn't sure I would find anything to begin with. However, I hoped that I might at least find out who was responsible for laying the traps. Often enough, being visited by a dragon was a fairly solid repellent to bad behaviors. Most people didn't think to lie when confronted with one.

Alas, I found only woodland creatures that belonged in the woods. Not even a hint of anyone sneaking around, up to no good. For all intents and purposes, the woods were free from humans for the day. At least none I was able to find. And I'm great at what I do. So, it stands to reason that if I couldn't see them, whoever it was either had the knowledge on exactly how to hide from me—which wasn't likely —or they weren't there. The latter was the more realistic option.

As I said, I'm great at what I do.

I supposed it wasn't a total loss. I was able to find a handful of traps and not only disarmed them, but I also tossed them into the small lake on the northern side of the region. A few less traps meant a few less injured innocents. Which was a win in my book.

As my shift ended, I started back for the castle and landed inside the gates. I shifted back to my human form and approached the door. As I reached for the knob, it opened, revealing Emily and Jax laughing and giggling like two hormonal teenagers.

"Oh, hey Bret," Emily said. Her face was red, and her hair was all over the place.

I narrowed my eyes as my lips curved into a smile. "Hey yourself."

"I was just leaving to relieve you," Jax said.

I nodded. "I'm sure you were."

Jax poked Emily in the side. She giggled.

That little sting of jealousy started to poke its way through again.

I cleared my throat. "So, what have you two been up to?"

Emily glanced at Jax. Her cheeks picked up a little more color. The way she looked at Jax, it was like her world revolved around him. I wanted her to look at me in the same way.

"Oh, this and that," Jax said. "Don't worry, the activities were all Marcus approved."

"I'll fill you in later," Emily said. "But you might get bored."

"Bored seems to be the theme of the day." I nodded and smiled wider. "I'm going to hold you to that."

Jax wrapped Emily in his arms, and the tiny, green bug bit a little harder. I rolled my eyes and tried to shove the sensation deep down. As far down as it would go. Then Jax turned her back to me. He smiled at me like a kid with his hand stuck in a cookie jar and all without a single ounce of guilt.

I glared at him. "All right, all right, you two. Break it up."

Emily laughed even harder. "Stop tickling me, dammit."

As much as I hated making her stop, I loved the sound of her laugh. It was like music to my ears. I could listen to her laugh all day. I wanted to be the one to make her laugh. I would spend the rest of my life doing anything and everything to keep that smile on her face if she would let me. All to keep her happy.

And unlike Marcus, I would refuse to let her go. Ever.

"He's right. I need to go…" Jax said as he let Emily go and then settled his gaze on me. "Unless you would like to pull a double."

"Not on your life," I muttered. His reactions told me he was aware what he was doing did to me, and I hated that he knew me so well. Whatever he did with his time with Emily, he was trying to rub it in my face.

It wasn't like Jax to want to blow off work, especially for Emily. But we all had missed her terribly. Her absence was felt in the air we breathed each day that she wasn't bouncing down the halls.

But that jealousy was getting the better of me and I took a deep breath in. She didn't smell like him, and he wasn't bathed in her scent. So at least he didn't have sex with her. It was a small miracle. Very small. It was only a matter of time before he lost his self-control and took her.

Not if I got to her first.

Jax laughed and clapped my arm. "Oh, come now, you know you love me."

"What has gotten into you?" I asked, glaring at him. "Since when do you joke around?"

He shrugged, holding his hands at his sides, about shoulder level. "Things are changing. And for the better, my friend."

I glared at him. He wasn't making a lick of sense. But I supposed I couldn't blame him. Emily had a tendency of making the people around her—particularly me—euphoric. But that didn't matter when we had a job to do. "You better be going."

Jax sighed. "I really do. Don't have too much fun."

He seemed sobered up. A little. Like the threat of me getting to Emily before he could had started bothering him. I almost chuckled.

Good. He should be worried.

Jax walked off toward the middle of the courtyard and shifted into his white dragon. He let out a roar which caused Emily to shriek and laugh seconds before he flew away. I turned to face the woman I had fallen in love with years ago but had remained out of reach thanks to being attached to Marcus. She leaned against the doorway with her arms crossed over her chest, smiling at me.

"So," I said, clapping my hands, "tell me all the juicy bits."

She laughed. "You're impossible."

"Maybe, but you have to admit you like it," I said as I walked through the door. Emily stood off to the side, allowing me through. "Besides, you promised."

"Maybe like it, and you're right. I did promise," she said and headed into the living room as I shut the door on my way through.

"Seriously, how was your day?" I asked as I followed her to the couch.

She shrugged. "It was fun."

"But was it too much fun?" I asked hoping I didn't sound to desperate.

She shrugged again and took a seat on the couch. "Maybe."

"I need the details," I said with a little too much gusto. I cleared my throat and added, "I'm dying to know."

She laughed. "Nosey much?"

"Possibly, but spill," I said and sat on the arm of the couch next to her.

"We finished the game, sparred, ate lunch, and then I took a long shower," she said.

"You're making me jealous," I said.

She laughed. "You'll live."

"I hope so. Can't leave you to deal with that dragon alone," I said, tossing a thumb in the direction Jax took off in.

It was nice letting my guard down like this. Normally it was my way of coping with uncomfortable situations. But this time was genuine. Real. And I couldn't get enough of it. Though I was fully aware she didn't have any thoughts of being with me when she first came around, it wasn't the same for me. I had feelings for her. Deep ones. Ones that had resurfaced with a vengeance with her return.

She was the only woman I could relax and just be with. There wasn't going to be another woman like her in this entire world who affected me in the way she did.

She laughed. "Oh no. Whatever would I do in a world without Bret in it?"

I chuckled. "Probably cry. Like, a lot."

She smacked my arm. "You're horrible."

I held up my hands in surrender. "Hey, I'm not the one who killed me with jealousy."

She laughed even harder before reaching toward the coffee table and picking up the remote.

"What are you doing now?" I asked, staring at the TV as she flipped through channels.

She shook her head and smiled. "Channel surfing. Obviously."

"I see that, but why?" I asked.

"To find something to watch," she said.

I nodded and looked around for signs of the master of the castle. "Where is Marcus?"

"Brooding in his room, like normal. Why?" She flicked her gaze toward me for a second before returning to her search.

I let out a sigh, exaggerating my shoulders slumping. "Go figure."

I stood up from the arm of the couch and took the seat next to her. She smiled and settled in, readjusting her position to face me a little more. The movement was slight, but I noticed. I leaned a little closer.

"So, what are you in the mood for?" I asked and gestured to the screen. "Comedy? Romcom? Thriller?"

"Wide range of options there," she said. After a few more moments, she added, "I'll let you know when I find it."

"Is it a surprise or something?" I asked.

She chuckled. "No. I'm just waiting for something to grab me."

"How about something scary?"

She stiffened. "Really? Are you new here?"

"Oh, far from it," I said and flashed her an evil grin.

Emily hated horror films. Ironic when you consider she was living with and had surrounded herself with shifters.

She shook her head, which made me laugh.

"What?" she asked. "What's so funny?"

"Nothing," I said and settled my attention on the flashing channels she flipped through.

"Seriously tell me," she demanded.

I smiled wider. "Nothing. Really, nothing."

"That didn't sound like nothing," she said.

I chuckled.

"Come on, tell me," she said, coming out with a tinge of begging.

"I still find it rather hilarious you don't like scary movies considering the company you keep choosing to keep."

She blinked at me. "Fair enough."

The controller landed in my lap. I settled my gaze on her, confused about what just happened.

She shrugged. "If you want to watch a scary movie with me, then you have to find one."

I picked up the remote and scrolled to the app button for the perfect selection. All the while with a victorious smile on my face. She was playing into my arms. And soon it would be literal and figurative.

Once I selected the perfect flick, I settled in and waited for her to lean a little closer. The second the movie's opening scene played out, she started sliding closer to me, little by little. With the third jump scare of the movie, she collapsed into me, burying her face into my chest.

I did what anyone would do in my position... I wrapped her in my arms and shut off the TV.

"What did you do that for?" she asked as she sat up to catch her breath and wiped away a strand of hair that had fallen in front of her face.

"Saving you from further upset," I said. "Marcus would be massively displeased and harder to live with if I ended up scaring you to death."

She let out a heavy sigh of relief. "Thank you for the mercy."

I chuckled.

Though part of me wished I had kept a hold of her for at least a little while longer. Then she sighed and leaned against me for a second before sitting up.

"What was that for?" I asked.

She shrugged. "I don't know."

I smiled, egged on by her action, and my cock growing harder by the second, I twisted in the seat and tackled her on the couch.

7

EMILY

I screamed as Bret collapsed on top of me. Though I had absolutely no idea what had gotten into him, I loved every second of it.

We wrestled on the couch with me bucking against him and feeling the rather large bump in his jeans press against my sex. Instantly my arousal hiked ten-fold and I bit my lip. The sensation pushed me over the edge. I wasn't able to hold back any longer. No amount of masturbation was going to ease the ache that was constantly throbbing inside me. Only one thing could fill that void now.

Without hesitation, I wrapped my fingers behind his head, pulled his face close to mine, and kissed him.

At first, he stiffened, as though he wasn't expecting me to make a move like that. Two seconds later, he relaxed and kissed me back, sliding his fingers into my hair and forcing his tongue along mine.

He was much rougher than I gave him credit for... and I didn't mind one bit. I felt safe with him. I've only ever felt safe with him, which made watching the scary movie with him all the better.

As his mouth ravished mine with an urgent need, I slid my hands down his back to his tight, round ass and dug my fingers in. Bret groaned, and the sensation sent chills straight through my soul. My arousal increased even more.

I tugged on his shirt, pulling it over his head and tossing it to the floor. Bret set up.

"Aren't you afraid we'll get caught?" he asked. "Marcus might not take too kindly to us having sex on his sofa."

I looked him in the eyes and shook my head. "I am unattached and can be with whoever I want. And I want you."

He smirked and undid his jeans, allowing his erection to slide between the zipper. My eyes fell to the girth and widened.

Dear God, he was massive. I figured he was well endowed, but my imagination did little justice to the real thing.

Before I had a chance to say anything, Bret pulled me into a sitting position. He gripped the seam of my shirt and lifted, gliding his fingers along my sides as my shirt rolled toward my head. Once the cloth was removed, he stared at me for several moments.

"You are so incredibly beautiful," he murmured.

I blushed and smiled. It had been years since someone complimented me in the way that Bret had just done. It felt good and left me speechless.

He laid me back down on the cushions of the couch and placed kisses all along my skin, starting from the part of my chest in between my breasts, and working his way down toward the waistband of my jeans. Without missing a beat, he undid the button and unzipped them before wrapping his fingers over the edge of the waistband and then pulled them off me. The air around me was chilly, and I couldn't wait for Bret to surround me in his warmth.

But instead of climbing back over me as I expected him to, he shucked off his jeans and lowered himself between my legs. My sex was dripping wet and aching with need, and the fact that his face was so close to it, I nearly orgasmed right then and there.

He raked his fingers along my thighs and planted kisses on the skin near the hem of my panties. He then shoved his nose into the cloth covering my sex and breathed in.

"You smell like heaven," he murmured against my sex.

"Thank you," I said through a shuddering breath. Goosebumps prickled along my skin and my heart hammered in my chest. He continued to kiss my thighs as his arms wrapped around them. His fingers slid underneath the waistband of my panties, and he tugged them off my waist and down my thighs.

"Well, what do you know? The carpets do match the drapes," he said and smiled up at me.

I chuckled. "Okay, weirdo. What did you expect?"

He shrugged. "With you, it doesn't matter. You always exceed expectations, and you always seem to surprise me."

"Um… thank you…" It came out sounding like a question.

He smirked and shrugged. "Just thought you should know."

"All right then," I said.

"Now, where were we?" he asked.

I leveled my gaze on him and arched an eyebrow. "Where do you think?"

He breathed in deep and smiled deviously. "Oh right."

He lowered his face to my sex and breathed in deep. He heavily sighed and spread my delicate folds with his fingers a second before the tip of his tongue brushed along my sensitive clit. I sucked in a shuddering breath.

"Oh… just you wait. I'm just getting started," he said.

His tongue danced along my sex. My thighs shook with the sensation. Pressure built between my hips as my orgasm started to build. I arched my hips and gripped whatever parts of the couch I could. My breaths quickened as he sucked up my juices from my swollen, wet pussy. Every motion caused the pressure to build and my orgasm to inch closer and closer.

As my orgasm started, his tongue slowed. My release flooded through me. And I moaned through my pleasure as he continued to push me through waves of ecstasy.

But he wasn't done yet.

Fingers dipped inside me stretching and filling me, preparing my entrance for his massive girth. As he shoved his fingers inside me, going deeper and deeper, another orgasm started to form. He hit all

the right spots inside me, coaxing the pressure to increase expo-
nentially.

Before long, I cried out through another wave of intense pleasure.

He pulled his fingers from me once my orgasm faded and lifted up
onto his knees, sucking off his fingers, licking every inch of my taste
from his skin. Then he smiled down at me and crawled over me. He
kissed the tip of my nose and then my lips as he settled between my
legs, the tip of his erection pressing against my entrance.

"I hope you're ready for this," he murmured.

"Sounds like a lot of talk and not a whole lot of show," I teased.

He chuckled. "Oh, darling, just you wait."

"Been waiting," I said, continuing to tease him.

He slammed into me. I clung to him as pain stabbed through my
sex, ripping me as he forced his way into me, filling every inch of
space I had available. From there, he took things slower as he moved
inside me and one hand braced on my hip, keeping me from moving
with him.

Once I was fully stretched to fit him, he released my hip and I
moved with him. I squeezed my Kegels with every thrust inside me,
relaxing them as he moved out. Over and over until he stopped.

His face hovered over mine. I met his gaze and he smiled. "You just
feel too good."

I smiled. "You do too, obviously."

He chuckled. "We need to change position."

"Okay, what did you have in mind?" I asked.

He pulled out of me and settled his ass on a cushion. He patted his
thighs, and I smirked. His cock stood erect with a sheen given by
wetness of my sex. I bit my lip, sat up, and then straddled him. Bret's
hands gripped my ass as I settled my entrance on the tip of his dick.

I met his gaze again and was startled by the intensity of the silver
in his eyes. Not breaking from his gaze, I slid over the top of his dick
and situated with him inside me. I ground my hips against his, moving
along his shaft with his hands gripping my ass, fingers digging into
my skin, urging my movements.

My orgasm started to build again, and I leaned forward to kiss him. My movements picked up speed and I buried my face into the crook of his neck, concentrating on keeping my movements steady.

All too soon, my orgasm hit, and I cried out my pleasure into his neck.

"There you go," he murmured into my ear. "Let it all out."

My body became weak, making keeping up the pace more difficult. But Bret helped, coaxing my movements again. And once my orgasm faded, he kissed me. His dick throbbed inside me as his tongue danced along mine. Then he leaned forward, gripping my breasts and massaging them before leaving my lips to suck on each one.

And just like that, I was ready to go again.

Though I had no idea what had come over my body since being back here, I was glad to have this moment with Bret. Sex with him was intense.

Bret's arms wrapped around me and squeezed me to him as he stood with me in his arms. I wrapped my arms and legs around him as he carried me from the living room and down the hall. It didn't take long for me to realize he was carrying me to my bed.

Once we were in my room and on my bed, he flipped me to my stomach.

"On your knees," he demanded.

I smiled and did as I was instructed.

His dick pushed into my entrance again, filling me completely just as he had before. Our skin slapped together, making a clapping sound. I gripped the comforter in my fists and lowered my chest to the bed, keeping my ass in the air.

Bret's arm wrapped around me seconds before his fingers brushed along my clit. Once again, another orgasm started to build.

He grunted with his movements, and I could tell that he was getting close, but instead of pushing through to his release, he stopped his movements to nibble on my back as he continued to massage my clit.

My orgasm hit, forcing me to cry out in pleasure once more. Though, this time, my cries were muffled by the mattress.

He pulled out of me and forced me to my back. Once he settled between my legs, he entered me. I widened my legs, wrapping them around his waist, allowing him to go even deeper. As he moved, he increased his force. The headboard on the bed slammed against the wall. He gripped my hands, holding them above my head with one hand as he wrapped his fingers through my hair with the other. All the while, he never lost a beat, maintaining the same mind-blowing rhythm.

As my next orgasm neared, his movements stuttered. He buried his face into my neck and grunted. My climax hit. Warm liquid shot inside me as he grunted and worked through each shuddering movement until they stopped completely.

As our orgasms faded, he pulled out of me and laid at my side. I rolled over, wrapping myself around him. We lay entangled together, catching our breath.

After several minutes, he sighed and announced, "I'm hungry."

"I'm tired," I said.

He pulled me into him, wrapping his arm around me and rubbing my side with the tips of his fingers. "You lay there, relax, and get some rest."

"Okay," I mumbled, closing my eyes.

I fell into the deepest, most satisfying sleep I had ever had.

8

MARCUS

I woke up with a start. I had no idea how late it was, but I was sure I slept longer than I intended to. I rubbed my face free of the last of the grogginess that overcame me and sat up in bed. Silence echoed around me, and I had a sense that something was off. I slipped into the hall, heading to the kitchen for a quick bite to eat. As I made my way, Bret slipped out of Emily's room and headed toward me. He nodded at me as he drew closer.

I glared at him.

"Where have you been?" I asked. "Better yet, what were you doing in Emily's room?"

"Entertaining our house guest," he said, smug. "You can take that as a blanket answer."

There was something in the way he had spoken the words which set my nerves on edge. I knew he referred to Emily. My more possessive side took over, following my raising suspicion that he was trying to take my woman from me, and I sniffed the air. What I breathed in ignited a rage inside me I hadn't felt in years. My eyes widened and I charged him while growling out, "You!"

Bret's back slammed against the wall, forcing him into the marble.

"You, of all people, would try to steal her from me! You know how

I feel about her. How could you do this to me?" I asked as I struggled with not killing the man who I had always thought of as a brother to me.

Bret didn't answer. He simply stared at me expressionlessly.

I couldn't believe him. I couldn't wrap my mind around how he thought what he did was okay. I pushed against him, taking a couple of steps back. I pointed a finger at his chest. "This is a new low, even for you."

Bret sighed, removing himself from the wall, and then readjusted his shirt and stretched out his neck as though he was getting ready to take me on. "I didn't realize she belonged to you. I thought she was her own woman and could make her own decisions."

"I would watch what you say next, if I were you," I warned. It wasn't going to take much more antagonizing for me to punch the man full in the face.

Bret smirked. "Well, at least now you know that Jax and I both feel the same way about her. Regardless of anyone's feelings, she chose me."

My fists clenched so tight my nails dug into my palms. I growled and pushed the man who used to be my brother against the wall again. "I'm warning you…"

"Look," he said firmly, "she chose me. If you want to take your rage out on someone, you should confront Emily. Though I wouldn't recommend doing that, seeing as how well it worked out for you the last time."

I sucked in a sharp breath and searched his eyes for an explanation for what he just said. I knew exactly what he was referring to. It was the moment I thought I had lost Emily for good.

She came to me after visiting with her family. Her mood was solemn, which wasn't like her. I tried to comfort her the best I could and coax out of her what bothered her so deeply.

I didn't like what she had to say.

Her parents promised her to the wolves. She told me she was going to honor their promise and that made me feel as though she was going to throw everything we had away.

I had confronted her. I was angry, hurt, and there was a huge part of me that felt betrayed. She was leaving me. For the wolves.

It was a moment that stung more than anything I had ever felt in my life. I thought of her as my mate. But I found out that day she didn't feel the same. If she had, she would have stayed.

But as time went on, I gained a better understanding of what she was doing and why. If she didn't go and uphold her family's agreement, she could have started a war. One in which her family would have been destroyed. Though I was sure a war with the wolves was a possibility even now that she was back.

That was something I would deal with when and if the time came. However, none of that mattered. Not anymore. And I realized Bret had a point. Mine and Emily's relationship ended long ago. We weren't together anymore, and she had the right to sleep with whomever she deemed worthy of her.

After several moments, my hands released Bret again. I stepped back and said, "You're right."

"What?" he asked as his eyebrows knitted themselves together.

"I don't have a say in who she chooses." I settled my gaze on the floor. "I had my chance, and I lost her."

"Hey, man, I didn't—" Bret started.

I turned my attention to him as my body flooded with emotions I thought I had put far behind me. The sensation of loss overwhelmed me. I could either kill him or surrender to the facts and accept that I had lost Emily for good. It was hard to breathe. And I hated that he made sense. But what could I do? It wasn't like she belonged to me. She didn't. No matter how much I wanted her to.

I took in several deep breaths to calm myself. Once those emotions started to fade, I nodded once and said, "Take care of her."

I gave up on finding something to eat. I was too upset. I needed something more constructive to do with my time. It wasn't like I was going to be able to sleep anymore, so going back to bed was out of the question. I took the only other thing that helped in the past and I turned around and quickly headed down the hallway.

Bret's footsteps followed after me. I tried to ignore him. The last thing I wanted was to deal with him anymore for the night. Especially with my feelings being so raw.

"Where are you going?" he asked, almost breathless as he was trying to keep up.

"I have to find the people hunting shifters before it's too late," I said, hoping he would take the hint.

Bret grabbed me by the arm, forcing me to stop. I turned around and faced him, settling my glare on him.

"What aren't you telling me?" he asked.

I took a deep breath and pinched the bridge of my nose. I understood better than most that he needed to know. Both him and Jax did. But I wanted nothing more to do with him for the night. Still, he needed to know. The best thing I could do was to put my feelings aside for the moment and tackle the growing problem that was rapidly getting out of hand.

Although, ideally, I would have done it with Jax present as well. Repeating myself wasn't something I was fond of. But I supposed beggars couldn't be choosers in this instance.

"Come on, man," he said. "What did you find out?"

"I went to see my friend, Chase, and his roommates. Emily had told me she stumbled upon some sort of meeting and found out the wolves were working with some humans. They mentioned Kai. He is one of my friends. The wolves are the ones setting the traps throughout the region."

"The friends with that one woman who found herself caught in a bear trap?" he asked.

I nodded. "The same."

"And?" he asked.

"Turns out he lost control over his shift and his girlfriend was too close. She died. Whoever the wolves are working for, it's got something to do with the girl's death."

"Where did she live?" he asked. "How far does this really go?"

"The family reside on other side," I said. "Kai came here on his own. As a way to start making amends for the girl's death. As far as I'm aware, whoever it is followed him here."

Bret whistled. "Man… talk about revenge."

"And years later," I added.

Bret leveled his gaze on me. His eyes were filled with shock. "You're kidding."

"No. I'm not," I said.

Bret shook his head. "So, what's the plan? Why wait all this time before coming after him? Especially if it was an accident?"

I shrugged. "That is the million-dollar question. My best guess is it has nothing to do with the parents but someone else who was close to the girl. I just don't know who. But I need to figure it out."

"What do you need me to do?" Bret asked, ready to jump to action.

I nodded. "Initially, I thought I would send you to the other side to speak with the family. But it occurred to me that they may not know anything about this. Our best bet is to find the humans responsible and get to the bottom of this before anyone else gets hurt. Maybe even confront the wolves as well."

Bret nodded. "Consider it done."

"Good," I said. "Let's get started then."

Bret smiled. "Where to first?"

"The wolves. If we can convince them to give us the information we need, we just might be able to stop a war before it starts."

"Yes, sir," he said.

We headed for the front door.

I arrived at the door first and pulled it open. I got no more than a step outside of the thing before my intuition prickled along my senses. We weren't alone.

"What is it?" Bret asked.

I held up my hand to silence him and peered into the darkness just outside of the gate. Shadows moved low to the ground. I sniffed the air and nearly sneezed out the offending odor of wet dog.

"Wolves," I said.

"Guess they beat us to the punch, eh?" Bret stepped forward. "Show yourselves, now."

I followed Bret to the center of the courtyard. The shadows drew closer to the gate and two human figures approached, stepping into view. It was the wolf alpha, Bryson, and his son, Rowan.

They glared at me.

My hands formed fists at my sides.

"Where is Emily?" Bryson demanded.

"Don't bother denying she's here," Rowan said. "I can smell her."

"She's no longer your problem to deal with," I said. "She has sought sanctuary."

"You can't interfere with the arrangement," Bryson said. "She belongs to my son. She is his property. Return her now or you will be faced with a war."

"We didn't steal her," Bret said, then added under his breath, "Filthy mongrels."

"What do you think her mother would say when she learns of her daughter's betrayal? Everything she fought hard to achieve will be null and void," Bryson said.

I shrugged. "The rules of sanctuary are clear. Neither you nor I can do anything about it. If her mother wishes to come to me and learn the truth, I will be more than happy to tell her."

"You can't keep her!" Rowan screamed.

"We can and we will," I snapped. "So long as she has sought refuge behind these gates, you cannot touch her again."

The wolves around them whimpered and barked and whined. Each of them moved as though they were anxious. But by the time I had connected the dots and saw the shadows moving toward the sides of the walls that sealed in the courtyard, it was too late.

Wolves launched over the walls that surrounded the castle and charged toward the front door. Bryson and Rowan disappeared into the shadows.

Bret and I exchanged glances and then shifted into our dragons.

9

EMILY

Chaos erupted through the air, waking me from my deep sleep. After several seconds of trying to figure out what was going on, I realized the loud sounds were from a fight. And it was happening close by.

I leaped from the bed and rushed to the window to see what was happening. My heart hammered in my chest, and it felt like my feet couldn't move fast enough. Whoever was fighting, it sounded deadly, and I hated the thought of my men getting hurt.

Once I reached the window, I pulled back the curtains and found two dragons fighting off an entire pack of wolves.

I didn't have to guess who was behind it. But as I searched the collection of wolves, none of them were Bryson or Rowan.

"Figures," I muttered. "Fucking cowards."

Rage filled me. The bastards not only followed me to the castle, but they were fighting off the men I loved dearly. I wasn't going to stand for that. Of course, part of my anger was directed at me. I should have known they were going to follow me here. I took a risk and involved the men which wasn't fair for me to do.

Though I knew full and well the dragons could handle themselves against a pack of wolves, these weren't just an ordinary pack. They were cunning and had extensive training when it came to fighting creatures and shifters much, much bigger than them. Bryson made sure of that. Plus, they were incredibly strong. More so than most shifter wolf packs.

And the evidence of such I was witnessing with my own eyes.

That wasn't to say my men weren't taking care of business. Bryson had a habit of underestimating his foes and overestimating his strength. The sheer fact as much hadn't blown up in his face yet continued to astound me. And despite how much more powerful my men were, they were vastly outnumbered and close to becoming over-whelmed.

Regardless of the tactics or strength between the wolves and the dragons, there was one thing I wasn't going to tolerate, and that was the stupid fight taking place in the courtyard. I was going to put a stop to it and make my position clear once and for all.

I quickly dressed into whatever clothes I could find in the dark and ran toward the front door. It was standing open, and the disarray of the fight filled my vision just outside the castle. I continued running. Once I stood on the ground of the courtyard, I stopped and sucked in a deep breath, and yelled, "Stop!"

No one heard me.

"I said, stop. Now!" My voice echoed above the fight. But still, no one listened.

I dug deep into my magic and conjured what I could muster. My hands filled with magic. I held them in front of me, facing each other, concentrating the power between them. A ball of white light formed, growing stronger with bolts of purple and blue lightning shooting within it. A grey smoke filled the orb, creating a storm.

When the ball was at a size no one would be able to ignore, I launched it into the middle of the fight. It landed with a loud boom, and the blast shook the air and ground. It exploded like a heavy artillery round. Wolves were thrown into the air in all directions. The dragons took flight. All of them glared at me.

I shrugged off the looks and faced the wolves. "If the alpha and his son want me so badly they would cause a battle with dragons, then the two of them can come for me on their own or let me be. Regardless of their actions or what you are trying to accomplish here, I'm not leaving."

The wolves stood around whimpering and growling. None of them wanted to move. My hands instantly filled with magic. "I said leave!"

One by one, each of the wolves turned their tail around and left the castle's property. I let out a deep breath. Tension drained from my body. Then I set my gaze on two of my men.

Bret and Marcus landed and then shifted back into their human forms. Both of them stormed toward me with equally angry gazes. I stood taller, angling my nose in the air. I regretted nothing. If they had listened to me the first time, I wouldn't have been forced to the extreme measures I had gone to.

They forced me to break it up.

Before they reached me, I turned around and walked back into the castle.

I headed straight for the kitchen and grabbed a glass of water. I needed it to help return some of the energy I expended with my stunt. Sleep also helped. So did sex, which is why so many rituals revolved around it. But those were for the witches higher up than me.

Footsteps filtered into the room. The silence thickened and I felt Bret and Marcus's gazes on me, boring holes into the back of my head waiting for me to turn around. I downed the last of my water and set the cup into the sink before turning and facing them.

They still had the same gazes on their face.

"Look," I started. "Before you say anything, I regret nothing."

"Do you have any idea what you could have done?" Bret said.

I glared at him. "Do you have any idea how little I care about the consequences of my behavior? I knew you two wouldn't get hurt. That's why I did what I did. Sorry, not sorry."

I started to walk away. Both of the men moved to block my exit. I slapped my hands on my legs. "Move."

"Not until you listen to reason. We aren't mad because you used magic," Marcus said.

"We're upset because you put yourself in harm's way," Bret finished.

I looked between the two of them. The seriousness of their gazes was also backed by worry. My rage and stubbornness faded, replaced by gratitude. I approached each of them. I went to Marcus first, wrapping my arms around him and lifting up on my toes to place a kiss on his cheek. Then I did the same to Bret.

"Thank you," I said. "I appreciate your worry. Though I'm not as fragile as you think I am."

Both of them sighed.

"Any of you wanna tell me what happened?" I asked.

"Do you really need to ask?" Bret asked. There was a sarcastic hint in his tone.

I shrugged then moved to the island. "Well, I have all night, so someone needs to spill."

Marcus and Bret exchanged glances before giving in and taking a seat at the island.

"This might take a while," Marcus warned.

"Again," I said, "I have all night."

"I'll start the coffee," Bret said.

Marcus started to explain everything while Bret made a pot of coffee. "Some weeks back, I received a call from a friend of mine that a woman who had stayed with them got caught in a bear trap. Not any regular bear trap, mind you. One specifically designed for shifters."

"Why would someone do such a thing?" I asked.

Marcus nodded. "My question exactly. I walked them through stabilizing her as I was busy with an influx of other patients needing help for the same thing."

"Oh my God," I said. I was already starting to connect the dots. This was what Rowan and Bryson were talking about the night I found them talking with those humans.

"It was obvious someone was hunting shifters. The appearance of these traps and their injuries had been increasing over the past few months, and there haven't been any signs of stopping," Marcus continued.

"Then I showed up and told you exactly what you needed to know," I added.

He nodded. "Your help put some of the missing pieces in place. Now we know that my initial suspicion was correct. The wolves were working with humans. Though I didn't suspect the wolves until you told me about the meeting, it makes the most sense they were behind all of this."

"Why do you say that?" I asked.

"Because those wolves are greedy little bastards," Bret said. "Bryson being the worst of them all."

"You got that right, and Rowan isn't too far behind him," I added.

"Yes, well, be that as it may, we now know who they are going after and that is all thanks to you," Marcus said.

Bret took a seat at the island. "But we still have a long way to go."

"Do the wolves know where Kai lives?" I asked.

Marcus shook his head. "It's only a matter of time until they do if they don't already know."

"Who are the humans he's working with?" I asked.

"That's exactly what we are trying to find out," Bret said.

"Kai said he killed his girlfriend years ago, shortly after he first started shifting. He lost control of his animal and she was too close to avoid the fallout. Needless to say, he banished himself from the other side."

"Oh, the poor guy," I said.

Bret stood up as the coffee pot finished brewing. I took the time to process everything I just learned. Minutes later, a fresh, hot cup of coffee was sat in front of me.

"Maybe we can do something to call off the attack? Talk to the family and smooth things over the best we can?" I asked.

Marcus shook his head. "Her family is likely not even aware of the attacks. Whoever is behind this, they were close to her."

"So, it's a blood debt... we're just not sure who is trying to collect?" I asked.

"Yup," Bret says. "Fun times."

"Well, if there is anything I can do, I will," I said. "I don't want to see anyone else get hurt."

Bret chuckled, and at the same time Marcus said, "We got it covered."

"What?" I asked. "Do you not want me to help?"

"We don't want you to put yourself in danger," Marcus said.

"I can handle myself, thank you very much," I snapped, words coming out sharp. It annoyed me that they were treating me like I was made of porcelain.

"We don't doubt that, but we also just got you back," Bret said.

I continued to argue my position. I could be helpful. They needed to accept it. But the men wouldn't have it. After an hour of defending myself and demanding that I help and being shut down, I gave up for the moment. I needed sleep.

In the morning we would revisit this topic.

"Look," I started, "I understand where you both are coming from. But I'm too exhausted to continue arguing. I'm going to bed. And that, by no means, should be taken as me giving in. We will continue this discussion in the morning."

"Very well," Marcus said.

"Good luck with that and get some good rest," Bret added.

I glared at the two of them. "Goodnight."

I stood from the island and headed to my room, frustrated to the core. They had another thing coming if they thought I was going to sit idly by and let them do all the heavy lifting.

Once I collapsed on my bed, I stared at the window until my eyelids became too heavy to keep open.

10

JAX

It was late, and I was growing bored. Little did I know that was going to change… And not for the better. But seeing as how I had no idea, it made little difference in my mood.

I was flying over the forest, searching for signs of humans. Dragons had stellar vision and I prided myself on being able to spot things from miles away, and I was confident I would find what Marcus and Bret weren't able to. But a strange stillness had settled on the woods that had my tensions running high. Shadows were thicker than normal, and it made searching for humans setting traps for shifters a bit harder than I had expected.

My senses prickled with danger.

Still, section by section, I searched the woods and shadows, and I found nothing.

Needing a break, I landed in a clearing and stretched my wings and neck. I raked my eyes along the area surrounding me, finding nothing out of the ordinary. But I still couldn't shake the feeling of something being out in the shadows, watching me search for them. Definitely not human, that wasn't possible. Humans didn't have the ability to cloak themselves in such ways. But whatever it was, it didn't belong. Minutes later, I launched into the air and looked for a cliff to land on so that I could get a better view of the section of forest. I remained on the cliff, focusing hard on all the land. It shouldn't be hard to spot a campfire or a torch or flashlight. Especially with my eyes.

The land before me was dark and still. But that sensation that prickled along my scales remained. There was much more to what was going on below me than my eyes were picking up, which would have been hard to believe if I wasn't living it. Tension grew within me as I struggled to place exactly what I was missing. The key to finding the humans who were laying the traps was around here somewhere. I just had to find it.

And then movement caught my attention.

I had barely caught sight of some shadowy forms shifting along the ground. It was too clustered and weird for it to be nothing, so I went to investigate. What I found had kept me busy for the rest of my patrol and then some.

I launched into the air and drew closer to the area where the movement had been. The scent of metal, sweat, and meat filled my nose. The scent was familiar and struck me as human. Though I couldn't reconcile the smell with the inability to spot them with my eyes from above, I continued until I found their camp.

Though it was hard to believe, the humans were not only gathering but they were moving through thick woods unaccompanied by any source of light. It was a smart move, but how they were doing it left me baffled. But one thing was for certain, when there was one group, there was more.

I returned to the sky and continued to search for more groups, now that I knew what I was looking for.

In the span of a couple of hours, I ended up finding dozens upon dozens of camps filled with humans stationed in various parts of the forest throughout the region. I was surprised I had found as many as I had, rather that they were able to stay hidden so well. It didn't make sense for me not to even sense them until I was right on top of them. The fact that I had was purely by accident. Or even maybe luck.

Regardless, the important thing was that I had found them. And not a single one of them were using light. At least no obvious source, which made no sense.

The rest of my night was spent figuring out how many camps were set up in the woods and how many people were hidden in the camps. I had managed to scare a few of them off, but not enough to make a real difference. And I was sure of the ones that I had found, there were many, many more I hadn't.

None of what I had discovered was a good thing.

I was forced to return to the castle just as the sun started to crest over the horizon, shining its light on a brand-new day. Normally, I admired the sunrise. But this time, I was filled with hopelessness over what I had observed throughout the night. Still, I had flown home, doing my best to admire the colors that filled the sky as the sun rose higher. As I arrived home, Marcus was waiting for me in the courtyard.

I shifted into my human form and greeted him.

"Morning." I stuck out my hand toward him.

"Anything to report?" he asked, giving my hand a squeeze.

I nodded, lips curving down at the corners. "I have plenty. But not here."

My eyes raked through every ounce of shadow that filled the woods surrounding the castle. With the happenstance of which I had stumbled upon the camps during my patrol, it was possible that a few might have been keeping watch over the castle, monitoring our movements.

If I had somehow found a way to avoid detection as well as the humans had, that's what I would do.

Marcus looked around us, seeming to understand the hidden meaning in my words. He nodded. "Let's make this quick."

I gestured for him to lead the way. "I'll try to make it as quick as possible. However, you may want to cancel your plans once you hear what I have to say."

"I'll make that decision once you're done," he said.

Minutes later, we sat in the war room as I tried to find a way to start. I was still having a hard time coming to terms with everything I had seen.

"Jax, whatever it is, you need to tell me," Marcus said. He sounded strained.

I settled my gaze on him. He wasn't strained. He was exhausted. He must not have been getting enough sleep with everything going on. I couldn't blame him. I nodded. Words wouldn't come, though. At least none that made sense. But after several minutes, I gave up and just dug into my news.

"I found camps. Human ones. All of them were stationed in various parts of the forest within the region. And I only happened upon them by accident."

"What do you mean?" He narrowed his gaze on me.

I huffed. "They aren't using light. At least no obvious, typical forms of light. But the movement of shadow was what led me to them."

"Where did you find them?" Marcus asked.

I picked up some red-tipped tacks and headed to the map of our territory. I started placing pins into the paper, marking where I had found the camps. Dozens of them were scattered throughout the entire region. How so many of them existed didn't make any sense. Once I placed the fifteenth tack into the map, Marcus stopped me.

"I get the point," he said.

"And that's not all of them." I turned and faced him. "It gets worse."

"Yes. You mentioned you stumbled upon them by accident..." Marcus said.

I nodded.

"And they aren't using a source of light?" he asked.

I nodded again.

He took the information and withdrew into his thoughts for several minutes. "That makes no sense. Humans can't see in the dark."

"No. They don't. At least, not until now." I shook my head. "I can't explain it. None of it makes sense."

Marcus nodded. "Troubling, indeed."

"Well, it's not all bad," I said. "I scared off a couple of groups of them. Not many. Certainly not enough to make a dent. But there were dozens of others I wasn't able to scare off. And I'm sure many others I wasn't able to find, but I'm positive they are out there."

"How many are we talking about?" he asked. "Give me your best estimate."

"At least fifty groups, and I am unable to tell you how many are in the groups themselves. The numbers varied depending on the group, and that was only from what I could tell. One had ten people. One had five. Others had more," I said and shook my head. "Hundreds, by my estimate. And that's not taking into account any groups I didn't manage to find or any other variables we haven't taken into account."

"Fuck me," he muttered. He ran his hand through his hair and stared at the map where I had pinned locations for all the human camps I could find. But I wasn't done delivering my news just yet.

"The most concerning part about this news is how close they are getting to your friend's house," I added.

Marcus's eyes settled on me. He stiffened and huffed. "Of course, they are. Any idea on when they may get there?"

"A few days if not sooner," I said.

"We're out of time," Marcus said. "Call for Bret. He needs to be here."

I nodded and went to do my bidding. With hope, and a good dose of luck, we can get on the other side of this mess before too many more lose their lives. Once I made it to the door, Marcus stopped me.

"You were right," he said.

I turned to look at him. "About what?"

"My plans," Marcus said. "We have to address this issue now. It takes precedence over everything."

I nodded. "Yes, sir."

I left the war room and headed toward Bret's bedroom. I passed by Emily's on the way and stopped mid-step to poke my head in on her. She was sleeping soundly and peacefully.

Seeing her made the tension melt. Somehow, she was going to be the key to everything working out. She had to be.

11

EMILY

I woke up earlier than I anticipated. Probably not much longer after the sunrise, judging by the soft light that filtered into my room. Even though I got a little more than a couple of hours of sleep, I felt fully rested… and much calmer. And I realized I couldn't hold against the men their desire to keep me safe. They were only doing what they believed was right in order to protect me. Though I didn't need protection, it was nice that they cared about me enough to provide it anyway.

I was too rough on them, and I was certain that me being back in their home was a lot to take in. So, as a way to smooth things over from our argument, I decided to make the men breakfast.

But first… a shower.

Thirty minutes later, I was clean and dressed and heading down to the kitchen to start on the feast I had planned. The castle was quiet as I moved. So quiet that my footsteps on the marble floor echoed. I figured the men were still sleeping.

The place was old but had many updates, such as the marble. It used to be all stone. The castle had belonged to Marcus's family for generations, and each one had made improvements to the place.

Marcus's improvements were the updated electricity and lights.

Even though I would have enjoyed seeing the castle in its original glory, I had always loved the place. Regardless of the changes throughout the years.

Once I entered the kitchen, I got started on cooking pancakes, eggs, bacon, and made a pot of coffee.

An hour later, the men started filing into the room, likely lured by the smell of breakfast. The thought made me giggle. I was still cooking bacon, and the aroma of the crispy meat mixed with that of the coffee made my mouth water.

"Whoa," Jax said as he entered the room. "You've been busy."

I turned around and smiled at him as he took a seat at the island. "Yep. But wait until you taste the everything. The work has been worth it."

He took a seat at the island as I turned back around to flip the bacon.

Bret and Marcus entered the room. Marcus headed to the coffee pot and poured himself a cup before sitting next to Jax.

"Smells delicious," he said, sounding a little groggy.

"Thank you," I said. "Did you sleep well?"

He snorted. "Have to sleep in order to sleep well."

I had arranged everything on the island so that the men could help themselves.

I pointed to the arrangement and said, "Dig in, anyway. I have more coming."

"Thank you," Jax said.

Marcus mumbled in agreement.

Bret leaned against the counter and eyed me suspiciously.

I met his gaze briefly and said, "What?"

A smile tugged on my lips.

"What's all of this for?" he asked.

I shrugged. "My way of saying sorry for last night."

I took the bacon to the plate sitting on the island and added the freshly cooked ones to the pile. I met Jax's confused expression.

"What happened last night?" he asked.

"What I want to know is what part of last night?" Bret added.

Marcus sighed, stood from his seat, and pulled me close to him. "We just want you to be safe."

"I understand that," I said to Marcus, then to Jax, I added, "I had to use magic in a not so elegant way to make a point."

Marcus retook his seat, he filled him in on the details while I returned to the stove, where Bret still stood.

"We had a visit from the wolves last night," Marcus added.

I smiled faced Bret. "You should eat."

"I will," he said then leaned in close and whispered, "Any regrets between us?"

I twisted to face him so I could look him in the eyes. His silver orbs were outlined in a band of stormy grey. Webs of platinum sparkled throughout. His gaze was intense and nearly took my breath away. Never mind the spike in arousal that flooded through me. I bit my lip. "Should there be?"

He smiled and grabbed a plate from the cabinet. It appeared that he took my response as answer enough, which was fine by me. I wasn't sure how comfortable I was in having a deeply involved conversation with him about the sex we had with Marcus and Jax sitting at the island discussing the "visit" from the wolves.

Without another word, he headed to the island and started piling food on his plate. Once he was done, he sat down and joined the conversation.

"Do you think they will be back?" Jax asked.

"More than likely," Marcus said. "But we have other problems to worry about right now."

I placed the last few remaining pieces of bacon into the pan. They sizzled loudly, drowning out part of the conversation taking place behind me.

"What's going on?" Bret asked.

"Right, we couldn't wake you earlier this morning," Marcus said.

"Well, I'm awake now," he said. "What's up?"

"Jax..." Marcus said.

I turned around and divided my attention between the conversation and the last of the bacon.

Jax leaned in close. "There are camps of humans all over this region. They're gearing up for something big. And what's worse? They're getting closer to Kai's cabin."

"Why would there be so many camps all over the region if they were only after Kai to begin with?" Bret asked.

"That's what we need to find out," Marcus said. "One of the many growing questions."

That piece of information didn't make sense. There was only one reason I would gather an army, and that wasn't to attack only one person but to take out many more. An entire group of people. I quickly connected the dots. Whoever was attacking Kai, it wasn't just him they were after but all shifters.

This stank of Bryson and Rowan, and the deal they made with the humans.

"Wait," I interrupted. "Does that mean the humans are hunting all shifters?"

Though I already knew the answer, I wanted confirmation of my suspicions.

Marcus leaned back in his chair. He thought about his answer for a moment before he said, "It would appear so. I suspect it has something to do with the deal the humans struck with the wolves. It could be for control over the territory... it could be something else. Regardless, that is something we need to get to the bottom of."

So, Marcus suspected the same thing I had. That didn't bode well. From what I could gather, Bryson was always up to no good. If he was going to start a war with the shifters, it was for something big.

"And I'm just now finding out about this?" I asked, growing angrier by the second. I clutched the spatula in my fist. "Why would you keep this from me?"

"I'm just finding out about this too," Bret said. "I highly doubt it was being kept from you out of spite."

"Well, whatever the reason," I said, crossing my arms over my chest and putting my foot down, "I'm helping."

"Not this again," Bret mumbled.

I glared at him.

"No, you're not," Marcus said.

"Didn't we go over this last night?" Bret asked. "I thought you understood where we were coming from?"

"Is that what this breakfast was for?" Jax asked. "I'm confused."

I shook my head. "Unbelievable."

"None of us want to see you be put in harm's way," Jax said. "We all want you safe."

"Oh, I understand everything now," I said, voice rising an octave. "So, you get to put yourselves in danger for me, but I can't do the same thing for you. You want to protect me, but I can't do the same for you?"

"Come on now," Bret said. "You know it isn't like that."

"Don't look at it as a double standard," Marcus started. "Because for us, it's not. We're just doing what we're supposed to do, and that's doing everything in our power to keep you safe."

I glared at him and his gorgeous face. "Well, then how am I supposed to see it? Because, from where I'm standing, what's going on is the definition of a double standard."

"We're trying to protect you, for starters," he said. His brown eyes pleaded for me to stop. He seemed exhausted and like he hadn't slept in a few days. Much more than just last night.This whole wolf, human, killing shifters thing has got him so deeply, he was losing sleep.

But that didn't mean I wasn't angry.

"I don't need protecting," I said, nearly shouting. I slammed the spatula onto the counter and faced the men. "You have another thing coming if you think I'm really some pathetic damsel in distress. Look, I found this whole thing cute for a while, but now I'm annoyed. I can fight. I can use magic. I can help."

"You're not coming," Bret said, firmly. I wasn't sure what bothered me more. The fact that he had spoken so calmly, or what he had said.

"I second that," Jax said.

Marcus met my gaze and shrugged. "I agree with them."

"This wasn't up for a vote," I snapped.

"Regardless, we all agree everything is too dangerous for you to come," Jax said.

I looked between the three of them. Meeting each of them in the eyes. My anger was starting to get the best of me, but I couldn't back down now. I refused to sit back and watch everything from the sidelines. Not when I could do something to help.

"All right, look, the three of you," I started. "I'm not weak, fragile, or incapable. I can handle myself, and I can help."

"No one is arguing your strength here," Jax said.

I held up my hand to stop him. "I'm not finished."

He nodded, holding his hands up in surrender.

"Either I help with your blessing, or I'm helping without it. Regardless, I'm helping," I said.

12

BRET

I stared at the woman that I had fallen hard for and was filled with enormous admiration. She was certainly a firecracker. And not because she was a redhead with curves for days and an air about her that kept me wanting more from her.

"You're being unreasonable," Marcus said.

I settled my attention on him. His eyes had darkened to almost black, and that was never a good sign. He settled his gaze on me in the uncomfortable seconds that followed. He really shouldn't have said that to her.

"Listen here, you stubborn, exhausting asshole, I am not the one being unreasonable," Emily said. "You three are the unreasonable ones."

I rolled my eyes and sighed. All Marcus had done was add fuel to the fire.

"I stand by what I said," he added.

"And I stand by what I said. Now, eat up," she said. "I'm going to go take a shower."

"We'll take care of the cleanup," I offered.

"What?" Jax said, voice flat.

I shot him a warning glare then said to Emily, "Go get all sudsy and fresh and whatnot."

"Thank you," she said. Her lips curved up slightly. Barely enough to make a smile, but close enough. "Are you sure you have this covered? I have no problems with taking care of my own messes."

Her eyes flitted to Marcus for a brief moment before resting back on mine.

I chuckled. "Just go, will you?"

"Fine," she said through a sigh and left the room.

"I highly suggest we be done with the business talk for right now," Marcus said. "We can pick this up after breakfast and we're done with cleaning the kitchen."

And quite the mess had covered the kitchen for sure. Emily had outdone herself. Doing the dishes was the best way we could all say thank you. Besides, Marcus was right. We needed to step away from the situation. The tension in the room needed to dissipate and our minds needed to clear before we could revisit the topic that was almost literally at our doorstep.

I had no arguments and continued to eat my breakfast. But my thoughts were consumed by what lay ahead of us.

The rest of breakfast was spent in relative silence. Most of the food was consumed, which was saying something. Jax might have been the smallest of the three of us, but he packed away more food than Marcus and I could combined.

And who could blame him? Emily was an astounding cook. I could envision the three of us becoming fat, full, and happy solely based on her food and presence alone.

Once I was finished eating, I stood from the island and took my plate to the sink. From there, I started rinsing dishes and placing them into the dishwasher. Once that was full, I started the machine and then got to work on handwashing the pots and pans and anything else that wouldn't fit into the machine.

When Jax finished his food, rinsed his plate, and set it in the sink. He took care of the counters and the island, scrubbing all the bits of hardened batter from the surfaces along with the stove.

Minutes later, Marcus joined with a broom and dustpan. He also packed away the leftover food, sticking it into the fridge for later.

"If she keeps feeding us like this," I said, "We're all going to get fat."

"That's what working out is for," Jax said.

"Easy for you to say," Marcus muttered. "You are hollow through and through."

"No kidding," I said with a snort. "You eat more than the two of us and never gain a pound."

"Only good metabolism," Jax said, smacking his gut. The smile furthered his point.

"The thing about metabolism is that it disappears with age," Marcus said.

"Oh, the doc is bringing out his medical expertise now," I said and laughed. "Enjoy this now, Jax. Your luck is going to run out sooner or later."

Jax waved us off. "Whatever. You're both jealous."

"Sure... sure...we'll go with that," Marcus said. "Just remember working out and you'll be fine."

Jax grumbled something under his breath as he continued to work.

About twenty minutes later, the kitchen sparkled. The three of us stood back and admired our handiwork, patting ourselves on the back.

"Let's head to the war room to plan," Marcus said and left the room.

Jax followed next, and I took up the tail with a heavy sigh. It was time to face the music and form a plan of action.

Once we made it to the room, we collected around the table that was covered with a cluster of papers. A map of our region covered the wall, and stuck inside it were several red pins that weren't there before. The pins drew my attention as I pulled out my chair to take a seat.

"What's all that about?" I asked, pointing to the map. "What do the red pins mean?"

"Those are only a few of the camps I found," Jax said. "Marcus had me stop before I was finished."

"How many more are we looking at?" I asked as I counted the number of pins. I stopped when Marcus spoke again.

"It's how he found them still has me worried," Marcus said.

"What's so hard about finding human camps?" I asked. "The fires and other sources of light generally give them away rather easily."

Jax shook his head. "They didn't use them."

"What do you mean by that?" I asked. "How did you find so many camps if none of them used light."

"By sheer luck and perseverance. It was only by chance that I found them," he said.

"And with luck, we can find more and figure out what they mean to do with us," Marcus added. "But not before addressing how close they are to my friend's home."

"Right. The plan," I said and tapped my fingers on the table. "How did you want to handle this? More dividing and conquering?"

Marcus sighed and leaned over the table, propping himself up with his arms. He turned his attention to the map on the wall and sighed again as he stared at it. After several moments, he finally said, "The only way I think we can do this is by patrolling the region all at once."

A knock sounded on the door. No one needed a guess as to who it was.

I looked at Marcus, waiting for his signal on what to do. He shook his head. I chuckled sarcastically. "You can't keep her under lock and key forever."

"I know I can't," he said.

"You were there for what she said earlier," Jax added. "If we don't include her and give her something to do, she'll find a way to help on her own and that could be disastrous."

"I understand that," Marcus said. His voice sounded strained. Almost as though the topic was trying his patience.

"Well?" Jax said.

"Don't worry, I'll let her in." I stood and walked to the door, gripping the knob and pulling it open.

Emily, stood on the other side with her arms crossed over her chest. "Took you long enough. Did you have to have a delegation on whether or not to let me in?"

"You're right on time," I said.

She smiled as I held the door open wider for her to walk through. She sauntered into the room, round ass swaying from side to side as she headed to a chair and took a seat.

"So, what did I miss?" she asked.

"Nothing really," Jax said.

"We just got started," Marcus said. "I mentioned the three of us patrolling the region all at once."

"Where do I come in?" she asked.

Marcus sighed. He pinched the bridge of his nose as though the idea of Emily being helpful was beyond him. I couldn't blame him to a point, but he wasn't going to win this one, and he knew it.

"Do I really need to repeat myself?" she asked. "I'm helping. End of discussion."

"The way I see it," Marcus said, continuing where he left off, "We divide the region into thirds."

Emily scoffed. "Nice."

Marcus leveled his gaze on her. "You will go to Kai's cabin and keep an eye on things there. Set up wards, or any other protective measures that you can think of. We need to provide a barrier around the property somehow. The hunters may be drawing closer but that doesn't mean we should make it easy for them."

Emily leaned back and huffed. "I know what you are doing, and I don't like it."

"This is the compromise," Marcus said. "Take it or leave it."

"Take it." She huffed. After several seconds, she smiled. "I'm already forming some ideas on what to do. Of course, I'll have a better idea once I'm there."

Marcus nodded. "I'll take the region covering the cabin. I can be close by if Emily needs me, and Kai is one of my friends. I feel as though I have a certain responsibility to them."

"Say no more," I said. "Jax and I will take the last two sections."

Jax turned his attention to me. He hated when I spoke for him. I loved doing it if only to see the reaction on his face. I wasn't disappointed.

"What do you think? Flip a coin?" I asked.

Jax pinched the bridge of his nose. "Does everything have to be a joke?"

I shrugged. "Not everything. But where's the harm in a little gamble for who takes what region?"

Marcus said, "You'll take the upper region."

"Party pooper," I muttered.

Marcus continued as though I hadn't spoken. "Jax, you take the last one. Be sure to debrief Bret on the other locations of the camps that you were able to find. With luck, we can find more and head them off."

"Will do," Jax said with a nod.

Marcus shook his head. "These aren't regular humans. They will likely stand their ground and fight rather than run and hide. We need to be prepared for anything."

"Especially since it's only a matter of time before they find the cabin," Emily said.

I smirked. Firecracker, indeed.

After a few final details, we were dismissed to prepare ourselves to leave. I stayed back with Emily and leaned in close, "You gave in on Marcus's plan a bit too easily, don't you think?"

She shrugged. "Maybe. Maybe not."

"What's going on in that beautiful head of yours?" I asked.

"Nothing. I just figured that beggars couldn't be choosers. I don't agree with the plan, but being stationed at the cabin is better than nothing."

"Interesting," I mused.

"It was the best way forward. Like Marcus said, it was a compromise and I needed to take it. That's all."

I pulled her in close and breathed in the scent of her hair. "Be careful out there. I can't have you missing pieces of your body."

She laughed. "You're ridiculous."

"Still, be careful. I would hate to see you hurt. Even a little bit."

"I'll be fine," she said and lifted up on her toes to place a kiss on my mouth.

If I didn't have to prepare for the upcoming battle and patrolling, I would take her on the table in the middle of the war room.

She smiled at me like she had heard my thoughts and pulled away while gently biting her lip. "I should go get ready to go."

"Must you?" I asked.

She giggled as she walked away from me. I sighed as I watched her head toward her room. Once she was out of sight, I went to do a little preparation of my own.

13

EMILY

A couple of hours later, I was riding on Marcus's back in his dragon form as we headed toward his friend's cabin. It wasn't much longer before we land somewhere near the cabin. At least, I assumed we were near the cabin. I hadn't been there before, but I knew Marcus would take me as close to the location as possible. Especially with how over-protective he was.

Once I climbed off of him, he shifted back into his human self and we walked together in silence, staying close to one another. The peacefulness of the moment reminded me of times in the past where we were content to enjoy each other's company. Neither of us wanted to fill the silence between us with idle chatter. It was a wonderful reminder of how amazing things were when we were together.

"So, this is the location?" I asked as a small cabin came into view, nestled between a collection of thin trees that towered high into the air.

Marcus nodded, keeping his eyes trained on the area around us. "I suggest forming the barrier from here."

We were a solid three hundred feet from the cabin. Marcus's suggestion was a solid idea. With how thick this forest was, setting up wards and traps too close to the house would give us too little time to react.

I nodded. "Excellent idea."

"I do tend to have those from time to time," he said.

I laughed. "Look at you being funny."

"I was being serious," he said and grabbed my hand. "Come on, let's get this started."

"Okay," I said.

We walked up to the door. Marcus lifted his fist and pounded on the surface a couple of times. A woman with long blond hair answered. Her bright blue eyes went from me to Marcus, and she smiled.

"Doc, hey!" she said.

She was very perky and warm. Her eyes complimented her long golden hair. Most of all, I felt an instant pull toward her.

"We have news, can we come in?" he asked.

"Sure," she said and opened the door to allow us through.

Once we stepped in, three men came into the room to greet us.

"Hey Marcus," one said. He had short brown hair and light hazel eyes. He approached us with his hand out.

"Chase, good to see you," he said. "This is Emily."

"Pleasure," he said.

"Nice to meet you, Chase," I said.

The next one was a beast of a man with long, light brown hair that shimmered in streaks of gold. His eyes were as dark as mud. His face was coated in a thick beard and his thick muscles rippled through his t-shirt.

"Hey Marcus," he said and settled his suspicious eyes on me.

"Kai, this is Emily," Marcus said.

"Nice to meet you," I said and stuck out my hand.

His gaze fell to my hand and then he met my eyes with a nod. I put my hand back to my side. I figured he wasn't the trusting type. Or a man who liked to shake hands.

"I'm Cassie," the woman said and approached me with her hand out.

I smiled and took it. "It's a pleasure to meet you."

"Likewise," she said.

The last one was big and burly with short blond hair and blue eyes. They were kind and smiled with his lips as he took Marcus's hand and gave it a firm shake. "To what do we owe the pleasure of this visit?"

"Jasper, this is Emily," he said. "And as far as the visit, I'm afraid it's not for pleasure."

"Oh?" he asked with his eyebrows forming high arches on his forehead.

"I'm thrilled to meet all of you," I said. "I wished it was on different terms."

Jasper nodded at me and looked at Marcus. "What's going on?"

As Marcus spoke to the men regarding the new developments in the hunters seeking Kai, Cassie pulled me to the side. "I'm so glad there's finally another woman around."

I laughed. "It does get lonely being surrounded by so much constant testosterone, doesn't it?"

She shrugged. "A little."

I could already tell that Cassie and I were going to be the best of friends. She seemed to feel the same connection I had with her instant charm and warmth, of which I found exceptionally refreshing. I had longed to have a woman in my life that I could befriend and hang out with. I hoped that this was the beginning of a beautiful, long relationship.

"She's a what?" Kai snapped, pulling my attention to him.

"Careful, Kai," Marcus said, holding up his hand to stop him from doing something he might live to regret.

"Relax, man," Jasper added.

"She's one of the good ones," Marcus finished.

"Yeah. Sure," Kai said taking a couple of steps farther away from us. He settled his glare on me as a pinch formed in the center of my forehead. I didn't do a damn thing to him, but apparently, he had some negative experiences with witches in the past. At least, I assumed that was the thing that set him off with me.

Cassie wrapped her hand around my arm and guided me to the couch. "You'll have to forgive him."

"It's fine," I said.

She settled her glare on Kai. "Not all witches are evil and vindictive."

"Thank you," I said and smiled warmly at her.

"Cassie's right," Marcus agreed. "We have bigger problems to solve right now anyway. But to do that, we all need to have cooler tempers."

Kai huffed in the way that made me believe it didn't matter who vouched for me, his prejudice against witches was deeply seated and it would take much more than votes of confidence to sway him.

"No, it's okay," I said to Marcus. To Kai, I added, "I don't care if you believe me or not. The only thing you need to do is sit back and watch."

He glared at me. Marcus held up a hand to stop me.

Standing my ground, I added, "No, he needs to understand that I'm here to help. I don't have some twisted, hidden agenda."

"Oh, you're my hero," Cassie said.

I giggled as I turned my attention to Cassie. "Thank you."

"Come, let's have some girl talk," she said as she took a seat on the couch.

Cassie and I continued to chat while Marcus wrapped up his little meeting. I already loved her like a sister. It was also nice to have someone of the fairer sex to talk to. She wasn't in the least turned off by my being a witch, and that made me love her all the more. In fact, it seemed like the only one who had an issue with me was Kai. And I didn't care to figure that out.

"So, tell me about you," I said.

"Where do I start?" she asked, still smiling.

I shrugged. "Do you have any family outside your men?"

She shook her head. "I have a younger sister. She's on the other side, living her best life with her men."

I nodded. "You must miss her."

"Every single day. I had to take care of her since our parents died, and one day I found some heirlooms and that was the last day I had to take care of her."

"Maybe we could go see her someday?" I offered.

She sighed. "I would love that. Now, what about you?"

"My family is an entire coven," I said. "Unfortunately, we're not on the best of terms."

"How come?" she asked.

I shrugged. "They arranged for me to be married to a wolf."

"Oh… that's… That sounds horrible," she said.

"Depends on the arrangement. Mine was. The guy was abusive. But it wasn't all bad," I said.

"How so?" she asked.

"The guy I was promised to is the son of the alpha of the wolf pack here. They are also the ones who were setting up traps for a group of humans in an effort to catch Kai." I threw a thumb in his direction. "I managed upon the information by accident, which in turn, brought me here to you."

"Wow," she said.

I nodded and smiled. "See? Not all bad."

"Kismet, right?" she asked.

I chuckled. "Something like that."

Minutes later, Marcus shakes the men's hands again.

"And there is my cue," I said.

"You're not leaving, are you?" Cassie asked as she stood from the couch with me.

I opened my mouth, but Marcus beat me to the punch. "She's staying with you."

Cassie smiled even bigger. "Yas!"

I laughed. "I'm only going to go see him out and get started on my work."

Kai grunted.

I ignored him.

"I'll give you a few minutes and then join you?" Cassie asked.

"I would love that," I said.

Her eyes brightened and her smile widened even more.

I joined Marcus at the door and walked out with him. Once we were about twenty feet from the cabin, he turned around and faced me. As he stared deeply into my eyes, he cupped my cheek. I smiled up at him. The urge to kiss him filled me. It was just like before. When things made sense. The days back then were much happier and less complicated. Not to mention much, much freer.

"Please be careful," he said.

"You too," I said.

"I'll only be gone a couple of hours," he added. "If there is any trouble, shoot magic into the sky. I'll see it and come back as fast as I can."

I nodded. "Don't worry about me. I can handle things here while you're out. Take your time. Come back in one piece."

He pulled me close and left a gentle kiss on the center of my forehead. I looked up at him and smiled right before I lifted up on my tiptoes and placed a kiss on his cheek. Seconds later, he pulled away from me and disappeared into the trees. A few minutes following that, his red dragon soared into the sky.

I smiled and then got to work. The first thing I wanted to do was set up wards. As I focused on my intention, Cassie rejoined me.

"Are you sure I'm not interrupting?" she asked.

I smiled. "Not at all."

"What are you doing exactly?" she asked.

"Setting up an invisible barrier around the property," I said. I felt the ward click into place and faced Cassie. "Now for the fun part."

"What's that?"

"Traps," I said.

Kai stomped onto the porch and grumbled loudly to himself. I settled my gaze on him and shook my head. "He's a fun one, isn't he?"

Cassie chuckled. "Don't worry. He's like this with everyone new."

"Oh, I'm not worried. I appreciate you letting me know it isn't just me though. Besides, if he steps out of line, I'll flick him with a bolt of lightning." I winked at her.

She laughed.

I knew beyond a shadow of a doubt we were going to get along perfectly fine.

MARCUS

I stuck around, flying low to the trees, long enough to make sure Emily didn't run into any trouble. I wasn't worried about the groups of humans heading for the cabin. I was more concerned with Kai. He had never struck me as the unreasonable type, but I knew less about him than any of the other men who lived in the cabin.

And as I had suspected, he stepped out onto the porch and was keeping a close eye on things as Emily went to work with setting up the wards and traps around the property. I didn't much care for the way he glared at Emily. Or how closely he watched her. Though I was sure it had something to do with Cassie, I wasn't willing to take off just yet.

If he had kept killing his girlfriend a secret, there was no telling what else he was hiding, and that didn't sit right with me. Still, I wasn't going to withdraw Emily from helping. Besides, she was the happiest I had ever seen her. But that didn't mean I wasn't going to keep a close eye on Kai. At least, until I was certain he was going to behave himself.

It didn't take her very long before she had the traps and wards set. Once she was done, she and Cassie headed toward the cabin, and I was set to continue on my rounds knowing she would have Chase and

Jasper to help keep her safe. Just as I was flying overhead, she looked up and met my gaze. There was a glint in her eyes… an emotion that made me want to stay. I almost faltered in my flight.

There was a time when it only took something as small as her gentle expression in her eyes and I would crater. Though that was the case as now, I couldn't leave the fate of all the shifters in this region to a war they had no idea was coming for them. Though I wanted to make sure they never knew what dangers were coming from, by stopping them before they got started, I couldn't do my job if I gave in to Emily. Even though that was exactly all I wanted to do.

I flew higher, leaving the cabin and Emily behind. If only for a short while. But even as I searched the trees, looking for signs of the camps Jax had found, Emily didn't leave my mind for long. Her persistence to stay in my thoughts made my job more difficult.

I had never seen her so happy and at home as I did while watching her interact with Cassie. I struggled to recall a time when she had smiled more. Especially when she was with the wolves and promised to Rowan.

That wasn't to say I had checked on her, but I had checked on her.

Briefly, and from time to time. I had made myself scarce, so she never knew I was there.

I knew I should have let her go, but she was too special. I cared for her too much, and her happiness meant the world to me. So, sure, I checked up on her during moments when I missed her like crazy and just wanted to see how she was doing. It was enough to take the sharper edge of the pain of her absence away. So, yeah.

But now she was back in my life, and I didn't want to let her go. I didn't want to spend a single minute without her in my presence. I wanted to give in to her unspoken desire and make her my mate. I should have done so years ago. I wasn't going to squander this second chance. I would show her what it meant to be happy. More importantly, happy with me. I was going to make her want to stay.

My thoughts had encompassed me so completely that I had lost track of where I was going or where I had been. I shook my head and landed in a clearing. Though I had promised the men at the cabin I wouldn't be gone for very long, I was only going to check the area and make sure everything was clear before coming back.

But I continued to war with myself. On one hand, I wanted to quickly return to Emily. And on the other… I needed to make sure we were all going to be safe. I needed to take a couple of hours at least to do a thorough enough check.

And yet, I could still feel the kiss on my cheek. The warmth that filled her lips. The emotion within the simple gesture. I doubted the sensation would fade. None of what she did to me should have mattered, but it did immensely. But I was doing no one any favors if I couldn't clear my head and do a thorough check of the area.

I shook out my head and took to the skies again. Each time Emily crept into my mind, I focused harder on the land before me, checking for movement and any hint of the hunters were making a move on the cabin.

A couple of hours later, everything checked out. How long that would be the case, I wasn't sure. The important thing was that I could finally safely return to the cabin. Once I did, I made sure to land outside the traps and wards Emily had placed. If anything, it would show me whether they were placed effectively enough or not.

When I stepped through, none of the alarms had gone off, and I noticed everyone sitting on the porch. I smiled to myself at how well Emily had done. She was not only efficient but effective as well. However, taking in the scene on the porch, it appeared Kai still needed to maintain his distance. He leaned against the outside wall with his arms crossed over his chest, keeping his sights trained on Cassie and Emily. Other than that, everyone seemed to be having a decent time.

I approached the porch as their attention settled on me. Everyone welcomed me back, and I joined them, nodding in hello as each of them greeted me. Emily patted the railing next to her and I took the spot, leaning against the railing as everyone returned to their conversations.

Then Emily leaned in close and said, "I've missed you."

I smirked. "Is that so?"

"Yup," she said. "You were gone for a while."

"How much?" I asked, trying to keep how much her words affected me out of my voice. "How much did you miss me?"

She nodded. "A lot."

I chuckled. "In that case, I should go patrol again."

She quickly slipped her hands around my arm and pulled me closer. "Don't you dare go anywhere, unless it's with me."

I chuckled. "Okay then."

I resettled against the railing. "How was everything while I was gone?"

"Good," she said and smiled. "I really like Cassie. It's nice having another woman to talk to."

"I'm happy for you," I said. "What about Kai?"

I leveled my gaze on him.

She shrugged. "He kept his distance."

"Good." I patted her hand.

"What about you?" she asked, twisting to face me. "How was the flight?"

"Everything is clear for right now. I'll need to do another run in a bit. I'll wait for a few hours though."

"I hope so," she said, sliding a little closer to me. "I'm not ready to let you go yet."

Being with her like this… it was almost like no time had passed between us. It was a reminder of what we had, what I had lost, and what I desperately wanted to get back. Whether or not that could happen, I wasn't positive. But I sure as hell was going to try damn hard to make sure I got as close as I could.

"Wanna go for a walk?" she asked. "I need to check the traps and maybe lay a few more."

I nodded and took her hand, wondering if this was my chance to get her back.

15

EMILY

It had been so long since I had as much fun as I had sitting with Cassie and her men. All we did was sit around, talk, and have a good time. The fun was a different type of fun though. Not like hanging out with Bret, Jax, and Marcus. Time with them was different, though I couldn't explain how. It just was.

Despite having a great time with my newfound friends, I missed Marcus. He had been gone for a few hours. I wondered if he had found anything while he was flying. Or maybe he was in some sort of trouble. I hated that he and the other two were also in danger, that this whole thing went far beyond an accident from a man during his first few shifts.

Marcus was right though. Bryson had a hidden agenda when it came to the deal he made with the humans. And I was willing to bet everything I had that he was the culprit to the war.

I was starting to get worried when he arrived on the porch. The second his eyes settled on mine I felt a pull toward him. One that I couldn't deny if I tried. And I knew this from experience because I have tried. Many, many times. Especially during the first few months of living with the wolves. Eventually, I gave up. Because why did I need to give up that feeling? It wasn't like it was going to go away.

As it turned out, the feelings I had for Marcus, and the pull toward him, helped me through a lot of long, dark nights, especially the more horrible, nearly endless days. The point was I learned not to fight the feeling long ago.

Marcus leaned against the railing next to me. I smiled at him as relief flooded through me. After sharing a joke and him threatening to leave me, I clung to him. The feeling of his arm pressed close to my side reminded me of how it felt to have his arms wrapped around me.

Cassie resumed the conversation with her men while Marcus chuckled and resettled himself against me. It wasn't much longer after that that I suggested we go for a walk. I had a hit in my intuition that I needed to check on the traps and maybe add a few more.

So that's what we did.

Ten minutes into the walk, I looked over at him and smiled. He seemed so at peace. Even with a stupid war looming over the horizon.

"What?" he asked, catching me watching him.

"You look happy," I said.

"I am. For the most part," he said.

"Yeah?" I asked.

"Yeah." He chuckled.

"What makes you so happy right now?" I asked.

"Is it really that hard for you to guess?" he asked in return.

I shrugged. "Maybe."

He stopped walking, grabbed my hand, and spun me around to face him. I met his intense gaze, and my breath left my lungs in a rush. He pushed me against a tree and slammed his mouth into mine.

The way he kissed me was intense. There was so much emotion behind the way his mouth moved with mine. My heart skipped a beat because it was almost as though he was kissing me for the last time.

When he pulled away, we gasped for breath, and he rested his forehead against mine.

"That's how much I've missed you," he said.

I chuckled softly. "Well, why didn't you say so?"

He shrugged. "Doesn't matter now."

He started to pull away from me. I caught his arms, preventing him from walking away from me. "Where are you going?"

"You made your choice," Marcus said, sounding resigned. "I'm trying to respect that."

The tone in his voice confirmed the suspicion I had of him kissing me for the last time. My breath rushed out of my lungs. I wasn't sure where this was going, but the idea of him never touching me again cut deeper than a knife. Panic started to fill my center.

"What choice was that?" I asked, voice cracking.

"Bret," he said. There was a hint of hurt in his word.

I shook my head. Words failed me. In a sense, I did choose him. But for only one night. "Well, I'm making another choice right now."

His eyes searched mine. I sucked in a breath and said, "Show me again."

"What?" he asked, taking a step closer. He hesitated, and I knew how much he warred with himself.

"Show me how much you missed me again," I repeated and never broke from his gaze.

His fingers dipped to the back of my neck and the base of my hairline. And much more gently, he brushed my lips with his. Slowly, the kiss deepened. My back pressed against the tree once more. A piece of bark dug into my lower back, feeling as though it would pierce my skin, but I ignored the pain because I was kissing Marcus. At least, for the moment.

He pulled away again, sighed, and then said, "I hope he treats you right."

I groaned. "Just because I chose him that one time, doesn't mean I don't have the right and option to choose you now. In fact, so what if he and I had sex. It doesn't change my feelings for any of you."

"You can't have it both ways," he said.

"Why can't I?" I asked.

"I don't want to share you with anyone," he said. "I want you all to myself."

"Stop being a stubborn, selfish dragon and ruining this moment.

I'm here with you, right now, and all I want is you. Don't take that away from me," I said.

He stared at me silently. Though his eyes gave the impression he considered my words, but something still held him back. He stood in front of me, covered by the dark, seemingly trying to reconcile my words with what he deeply wanted, and I wasn't sure if this was the end of what we had.

The thought broke my heart.

"Stay with me," I said, more resigned than I wanted to sound. "Please."

A rush of breath left his lungs as he slowly closed the gap between us. His fingers gently grazed my sides as his hands moved to the small of my back. With less than an inch between us, he kissed me again. I couldn't shake the feeling this was the last time we would be like this. But instead of being wrapped up in worry, I decided to be present and enjoy the moment. I would worry about the fallout later. Besides, he was giving me exactly what I needed, and what he wanted.

Then his fingers dipped underneath the hem of my shirt. I moved my arms out to the side and allowed him to remove my shirt. Once it was cast to the earth beneath our feet, I pulled off his t-shirt.

We continued to take turns undressing each other as we threw caution to the wind and gave into our desires. Even if it was only for one night, or the moment. Even if the war took us from this life. Even if this was our only chance to be together. I was taking it.

Once we were fully naked, Marcus pressed me against the tree again. He kissed me once and stiffened as he pulled his mouth from mine.

"What's wrong?" I asked.

"You're not going to disappear on me again, are you?" His eyes met mine and held me captive within them.

My heart broke a little more. Tears stung at my eyes. "Not if I can help it."

"Good, because if we continue… there will be no letting you go," he said.

He kissed me again, igniting my skin on fire. His hands brushed along my skin, setting my nerves on edge. Everything he did made my arousal heighten. Then his hands went to my ass and squeezed me closer. His erection pressed against my thighs while his mouth moved along my neck and collar bone.

I hiked up a leg, wrapping it around his waist as he pressed himself into me. This time, his erection pressed against my entrance. My sex became flooded with anticipation. His mouth ravished mine and I relaxed into him, letting him do whatever he wanted.

His hand plunged between my legs. The tips of his fingers brushed along my sensitive clit. I sucked in a breath and shuddered against him. A few more strokes and I gripped his hard cock in my hand, sliding the length of him along my palm.

He rested his head on my shoulder, into the crook of my neck, and groaned. I smiled, egged on by his reaction from my touch.

Our mouths met again, kissing each other deeply as we continued to stroke and rub our way closer to release.

Within minutes, I sighed and shuddered against him. He stopped rubbing and pulled away from me, taking my hand that held his cock and tugged me away from the tree. He brought me closer one more time and kissed me before he gently coaxed me to the ground.

Dirt and leaves filled my nose as my head rested on a collection of pine needles and leaves that had fallen from the trees surrounding us. Marcus climbed over me and settled between my legs, and his erection resting against my sex, furthering my arousal.

He kissed my nose and then my lips, followed by my chin before moving his way toward each breast. He took them into his mouth, one at a time, and sucked on my nipple, gently raking his teeth along the tip. I ran my fingers through his hair as he continued to ravish me.

The pleasure in what he did made my toes curl. I was so wet that I was sure he was going to make me implode.

As he continued on his way toward my sex, leaving a trail of kisses to mark his path, I started to shiver with need. His hot breath poured over my delicate mound, and I sighed. My orgasm was so close I could almost taste it.

He slid his tongue between my folds, brushing along my sex before pressing his mouth fully along my clit, sucking and licking. My thighs shook and I couldn't catch my breath. Within seconds, I came, crying out my pleasure through the woods.

No sooner than my climax had ebbed, he climbed on top of me and pressed his dick into my entrance, gliding inside me with ease. He then lifted my legs to his shoulders before leaning over me. With a single push, I was thrust into wave after wave of ecstasy.

"You're mine now," he grunted. "You belong to me."

I wanted to argue that I didn't belong to only him, but words failed me. My mind was dizzy with pleasure, and I couldn't think straight to form any semblance of a sentence. Instead, I absorbed all the things he did to me.

Warmth bled through my body, almost as though my insides had ignited, but it was a pleasant sensation that washed over me.

And that made me cocky.

Pun intended.

I removed my legs and ignored the confused expression on Marcus's face and sat upright before I forced him to his back. Once he was laying down on the ground, I straddled him and allowed his dick inside me.

With circular motions from my hips, I moved above him, bracing myself on his chest. His hands explored my exposed skin until they rested on my breasts. My climax started to rush forward as his thumbs brushed along the tips of my nipples.

I leaned up, bracing myself on his legs at the spot below his knees, and rocked against him, letting my climax continue to build. Once it hit, I sat up and continued to ride him through the next wave of pleasure, crying out into the night air.

Just before my climax ended Marcus sat up and wrapped his arms around me. I moved my legs, wrapping them around him. His mouth connected with mine as we moved together. His dick throbbed inside me, and I gasped each time.

He groaned into my neck. As he moved within me, another climax started to build. Each breath and each move brought me closer and closer. Without missing a beat, he continued to move within me, placing kisses along my neck, holding me close to him.

His movements were slow and steady, which I appreciated. But there was a certain intention behind each motion. Everything he did had a purpose. And each one edged me ever so slowly to an orgasm. And it made perfect sense. He was as gentle and patient as he was in everything else he did.

But there was something sweeter behind what he was doing. And a hunger that could only be satisfied by me.

I wrapped my arms around him and dug the tips of my fingers into his skin. His mouth brushed the skin just behind my ear. Goosebumps prickled along my skin. I sighed.

Marcus squeezed me closer, forcing me to my back. "I can't hold out much longer."

I nodded.

He slid his arms underneath me and wove his fingers into my hair. They curled as he clutched my hair into his fists. Another rush of warmth bled through me. Comfortable and arousing.

I edged closer to my release.

I took in a deep breath as my climax hit. I cried out in pleasure as Marcus continued to control his movements, pushing me through wave after wave of intense release. He stiffened and grunted with each movement. Hot liquid spilled inside me as he continued to move through our shared release.

Once his movements faded, he relaxed above me, leaving a kiss on my shoulder.

"That was better than I had imagined," he whispered.

I chuckled under my breath. "That was the most erotic, amazing sex ever."

"Good," he muttered. "Don't you ever forget it."

I sighed. "I don't think I could."

"I also meant what I said," he added.

I met his serious gaze. "Which part?"

"You belong to me now. There is no going back," he said.

I smiled and kissed him once. "Guess you'll have to learn to share then."

He growled.

I laughed.

He really made it fun to goad him on. But there was a seriousness in my words that I hadn't realized was truly there. I could only see us working out in one way, and that was if I could have all three of them. Him, Jax, and Bret.

For me, there was no question. The problem was if three, hot as hell, possessive dragons could learn to share.

16

JAX

Boredom was not my thing. And I was miserably full of it.

After having done enough rounds of my patrol that I had grown dizzy, I landed on a mountain clearing that was high enough I could keep a bird's eye view of the world below me. But the forest was filled with a whole lot of nothing, and I had grown tired of my watch.

For such a dire situation, there was a lot of hurry up and wait. And that wasn't necessarily my team's fault either. There was too much waiting for my taste. And with not so much as a hint of something happening—movement, lights, anything—I was growing tired.

Sleep had been a fleeting thing as of late and the exhaustion was catching up to me. Though I understood I needed to stay alert, my eyelids grew heavy. However, what rest I could get was spent dreaming of Emily.

My thoughts became full of the fiery redhead that had captured my heart and attention as my mind tried its best to lull me off to sleep.

Things finally felt normal with her back in our lives. Like old times. But so much better. Though she was always beautiful, she had become even more so in her absence. Rowan, or whatever his name was, didn't realize what he had. And to treat her like she was no better than the dirt under his feet.

The idiot.

If I was ever lucky enough for him to come my way, I was going to make sure he knew exactly what he did, how wrong his actions were, and then I would ensure that he didn't have the ability to lay another finger on someone else again. Especially Emily.

The image of her smile came to mind. How warm and bright it was. And the way her eyes crinkled at the sides when she laughed as well… How could anyone ever do anything except love her and maybe even worship her just a little bit.

Okay, a lotta bit.

She deserved to be worshiped. That and so much more.

Man, I thought we had lost her forever. I had never been more grateful she was back. She would likely never know the impact her presence had on the three of us men. Especially Marcus. He wasn't the same after she left. It was hard to watch the man I had looked up to and considered my brother struggle with her absence in the way that he had.

Maybe someday, hopefully soon, we can all be open about our feelings. Then she might decide to stay and never leave. At least, never again. Not like in the way she had the last time. We could be free together, and happy.

I let out a wistful sigh as my eyes narrowed on the woods. My eyelids were becoming hard to fight. And just as I was about to let them win, a strange glow caught my attention.

I widened my gaze and studied the area a little more intently. There was nothing but tree and shadow. No movement. Nothing out of place. I figured the light was not only a figment of my imagination but a result of my exhaustion. And with a shrug, I returned to my thoughts of Emily.

That was until the strange thing happened again.

This time it was a soft bluish light that flickered in my periphery. Farther away than the last blip that had caught my attention. The object was only visible if I didn't look directly at it.

Several more appeared throughout the woods. Flickering and blinking in and out of sight.

I huffed a frustrated sigh. My thoughts of Emily would have to wait. I had some investigating to do, and if my intuition was right, I wasn't going to like what I was about to find.

I stretched my wings and climbed back to my feet. Dots flickered more and more. The lights filled a good portion of the woods. All moving toward the Cabin. That didn't bode well.

I launched into the air and flew close to the area where I had last seen the lights. I stayed close enough to the treetops I could keep an eye where the dots were appearing and low enough I could gain a solid idea of what I was dealing with. Hopefully, with luck, whoever was responsible for all the lights wouldn't be able to see me, and that was where I held all my cards.

I was a white dragon. And taking into consideration that I would normally stand out at night, especially one with as clear of a sky as the night was, which was also unusual for this particular region, I had learned how to keep myself hidden. A sort of cloaking ability, so to speak. Not every dragon has the ability, just like not every dragon needed to keep themselves hidden. But for ones like myself, it came in handy. Particularly on nights with a lot of recon, such as this one.

At first, I wasn't able to find a thing. Not even the human camps, which made sense. They were likely on the move and wouldn't be where I had last seen them. I probably would have been more surprised had they had remained in place. But I had a feeling whoever was responsible for the light, not only did they still lingered out of sight, but I suspected they were one and the same with the camps. I just had to catch them at the right time to be certain.

And so, I did. In the matter of fifteen to twenty minutes, I came to a collection of… something in the form of moving shadows. Though one might suspect shadowy figures in the middle of the night, within the heart of a forest, these were different. Like the night had taken on an essence and life of its own. If I had hair, it would rise on the back of my neck. But scales didn't work that way. Nevertheless, I couldn't shake the unnatural chill that covered my entire body.

What was worse, there were dozens of them.

I needed to get a better look, even though a move like that would require me getting closer and reveal my presence. That was a risk I needed to take. But whatever was moving below me, they were moving faster than what seemed normal… and in the direction of where Marcus's friends lived.

I had minutes to act before I would be too late to do anything to stop the marching army. It was do or die time.

Swooping in closer, I angled myself toward the ground until I got a clear idea of who I was chasing. I gasped as I realized I was following the wolves. How the wolves had managed to get so much speed or be able to use whatever lights I had observed remained to be discovered. The important thing was I had just learned that the wolves are behind the attacks, the traps, and they had grown in numbers beyond what we had anticipated.

A howl ripped through the night air. The shadows broke off in different directions. Except for the group in front of me. They had turned around and ran toward me. I landed and faced the group of dogs head on.

The plan was simple enough… in theory. I needed to take care of this group and chase after the others before they caught Marcus and Emily by surprise. Because I was certain the tactic the wolves had just pulled was a way to stop me with this smaller group, giving the larger one time to get to where they were going. The only hitch was, they had strengths I had yet to figure out. Abilities that wolves shouldn't have possessed.

As I stared down the small group of wolves growling and nipping at the air toward me, I sucked in a breath. Ice filled my throat. I held onto my magic, letting it form a ball. But the wolves, it seemed knew what I was up to and had grown impatient and attacked. Sharp claws and teeth bit into my legs and tail. I managed to keep my wings from being torn but then a wolf climbed on to my back.

I was overwhelmed.

Two more wolves joined their buddy on my back and more teeth sank into the back of my neck. I roared, releasing the ball of ice into the air.

A rush of fury set my nerves on fire. Now they pissed me off.

I flung my neck back and stomped my feet, twirling to fling the wolves off me and get the ones that were at my feet to back off. The wolves on the ground flew through the air in all directions. The ones on my back seemed to have had a good enough hold on my scales that they hung on. I barely caught the sight of one wolf who landed against a tree trunk with a yelp and a sickening crunch. His body fell to the ground in a lifeless lump.

I roared as I continued to fight off the wolves on my back. In the distance, a howl returned my roar. The rest of the wolves leaped from my back and fled, likely rushing after their friends.

But I refused to let them get away so easily. In fact, I had to do something about the whole group.

I launched into the air as magic filled my throat again. I was going to do the only thing I could to buy some time. Then I was going to find Bret and head for Marcus. With luck, we would arrive at the cabin before the dogshit hit the proverbial fan. Preferably with time to catch the army by surprise.

Keeping low to the treetops, I launched balls of ice toward the ground. When that caused a lot of destruction to the forest, I let loose my icy mist. A few yelps echoed through the air, signally I had found at least the ass end of the group.

I continued to circle the area until I was sure I had made a large enough dent in the collective and it was safe to go find Bret. Half the forest was covered in my magic and a collection of whimpers and high-pitched yelps filled the air. That was good enough for me.

I tapped into my strength, digging deep into my core, and put all the force I could muster into my speed. Not much longer and I entered Bret's patrol area. I roared as I flew, hoping to catch his attention just in case he fell asleep on duty.

Minutes later, and with no luck finding him, I had run out of time. I spent too much of it already searching for the black dragon. I turned and started heading toward the cabin as Bret flew to my side. Relief filled me. I nodded at him. He returned the gesture, and we took off in the direction of the cabin.

With our friends in danger, time was against us. We needed to make it to the cabin soon before it was too late.

17

EMILY

Marcus and I were cuddling and basking in the afterglow of our sex. I smiled to myself. The night was cold, yet peaceful. The forest was still. Not even the small creatures made a sound. Everything was perfect.

My eyes started to draw close as sleep beckoned me. Marcus's breathing was slow and rhythmic. His heartbeats drummed in his chest at an even beat. I couldn't recall a time when I was more relaxed.

Just as I started to drift off to sleep, a trap had gone off. I felt it like a tug deep in my gut, followed by a rush of warmth. I shot upright the next second. From somewhere in the dark came painful screams that echoed through the night.

Marcus sat up and groggily asked, "What's wrong? What's going on?"

"One of my traps was triggered," I said, standing from the ground and dusting off the debris from my body.

Marcus instantly stood and started helping with collecting the clothes. He tossed mine to me. "We have to hurry."

"I know," I said as I started pulling each article on as we headed toward the cabin. Another trap triggered, taking my breath away. More screams echoed through the night.

"What type of traps did you lay?" Marcus asked as he started pulling his clothes back on.

I shrugged. "The deterrent kind. Why?"

"They sound like they're dying," he said.

I shook my head. "No, but they probably aren't happy about being strung upside down by invisible ropes though."

He smirked which changed into a chuckle. He shook his head. "Clever."

I smiled. "Thank you."

Marcus finished dressing and took off in the direction of the cabin. I stared after him as his form disappeared into the darkness.

"Marcus," I shouted. "Wait for me."

"I'm here," he said.

I pulled my shirt over my head and then followed the direction of his voice. "Where? I can't see you."

"Shit," he said about twenty feet in front of me. "We're too late."

"What?" I asked as I barely caught glimpse of his form in the shadows of the woods.

"Stand back," he said.

I took several steps backward. Marcus shifted into his dragon, he turned around and headed toward me, flapping his wings as he moved slowly, gliding a few feet off the ground. Once he reached me, he picked me up and carried me over the trees the couple of hundred feet that was put between us and the cabin.

I glanced down at the ground below and caught sight of a sea of wolves and humans surrounding the cabin. They all moved restlessly within the shadows of the trees. I gasped at the sheer number of them. Resolve settled in my nerves as we descended toward the yard in front of the cabin.

Marcus dropped me off before landing, taking a guarded stance behind me while I faced the enormity of foes, all surrounding us. A mixture of human and wolf faces stared back at me. I stood taller, holding my nose a little higher in the air.

Marcus let out a roar, and sparks flew from his mouth. Not a single body trembled. I was surprised the humans didn't so much as cower or flee. Normally they would have. The fact that they kept their ranks told me we weren't dealing with amateurs.

I set my gaze into a glare and screamed, "Trespassers!"

A collection of stomps rumbled on the porch and the screen door slammed. I glanced over my shoulder and noticed Kai, Jasper, Chase, and Cassie had arrived on the porch. Cassie's eyes were wide. She flitted them to me briefly before settling back onto the crowd.

I did the same, just in time to catch some movement within the ranks. It was like the crowd separated to let one person through. A human. He stood tall, carried himself well. But there was a crazed sort of look in his eyes as he stared at the dragon behind me. He had long dark brown hair that looked unkempt, which matched the stubble coating his face. A layer of dirt stained his skin.

"Stop right there," I demanded. "Not another step or I will blast you into oblivion."

He acted as though I hadn't spoken to him and pointed directly behind me. "Come out Kai. Face your retribution."

"He's not going anywhere with you," I said, stepping in the way of his view. "Leave. Now."

I glanced over my shoulder at Kai. He glared at the man who stood in front of the crowd. His arms were crossed over his chest, and he shook his head. "Collin. So, you're the one behind all of this?"

"Wait, you know him?" Chase asked.

"He's my ex-girlfriend's brother," Kai said. "Does your family know what you are doing?"

"Does it matter? I'm making a stand. One against all shifters. Your people not only took my sister away, but you took my woman away as well. You twisted and corrupted her, and I demand revenge," Collin said, spittle flying from his mouth with some of his words.

Just then Bryson appeared and stood in front of Collin.

"Well, it's nice that you finally made an appearance instead of sticking your tail between your legs and running off before the action," I said.

Bryson glared at me. I squared my shoulders.

He turned his attention to Collin. "We made a deal. You will honor it."

Collin barely glanced at the alpha. He waved the man off and took a couple of steps forward. Bryson wouldn't let it slide though. He followed Collin and made the man face him by stepping in front of him, making the human stop in his advance.

Just as well. I wasn't one for empty threats and was ready to demonstrate how serious I was if he continued to push the issue.

"I'm talking to you," Bryson said.

"Well, I'm done talking to you," Collin argued.

"We had an agreement. You must uphold it," Bryson added.

I was impressed Bryson was holding his anger in control as much as he was. Then again, maybe there was something behind it. Whatever Bryson got out of his end of the deal it was major. Or maybe there was something Collin was holding over Bryson's head. That would be interesting.

However, I couldn't get a hold of that information just with what was said so far. More importantly, Collin seemed rather unmoved.

"You will uphold your end of the bargain or me and my pack will leave," Bryson said. "Trust and believe, you don't want to break a deal with me."

Collin smiled. He was quite handsome if he wasn't so psychotic. Maybe that's why he lost his woman. If Kai hadn't killed his sister, I wondered if Collin would still be here, trying to start a war he didn't have an iota of hope of winning.

"Go ahead and leave then if you must. Do as you please for all I care. I got what I needed from you anyway."

Rowan stormed to his father's side. "I am not going anywhere without her."

He pointed at me. I scoffed.

"Excuse me?" I asked.

"You belong to me," he snapped. "You are mine. You will return with me."

Marcus growled.

"I belong to no one, least of all, you," I snapped.

Marcus nudged me with his arm.

I looked at him. "What?"

He glared at me, and I realized what I had said.

"Can we talk about this later?" I asked.

He nodded once.

"Your family promised you to me, not these dragons. Come with me now and I'll forgive this slight. Stay and you'll never see your family again," Rowan said.

Fire encompassed me. "Say that again, little prick."

He growled. "Watch your mouth."

"Make me," I snapped.

He smirked. "I'm not leaving without you."

I stood my ground, hands filling with fire. "Over my dead body."

Marcus growled in agreement.

Rowan smirked. "So long as you leave with me, that's fine by me."

"Rowan," Bryson snapped.

Rowan glared at his father. "I said what I said."

"One problem at a time," the alpha said. "Starting with this one."

He nodded toward Collin who rolled his eyes before resettling them on Kai.

"Listen to Daddy, mutt," I said. "Run along now before you get hurt."

Rowan huffed. "You're going to pay for that."

I stood straighter with my nose angled into the air. If it was a fight he wanted, it was a fight he was going to get, and this time, I wasn't going to hold back.

18

BRET

I was busy on patrol, trying to follow some fleeting shadows which had continuously evaded me regardless of how close I got to them. It was the darndest thing. I couldn't figure out what or who was responsible for making the shadows, much less how they were moving so fluidly. No matter how many times I had tried to catch up to them, they escaped me. I was growing frustrated and there was no end to that in sight.

Jax's roar ripped through the night air. It sounded urgent. With a frustrated sigh, I gave up my hunt and headed in the direction of the sound. I had a feeling we were too late to head off whatever army that was moving in the direction of the cabin. I assumed the shadows were a part of the fight we had been preparing for. But I couldn't reconcile what I saw with what I already knew.

Wolves didn't have the ability to move so fluidly. Neither did humans. Other, darker things had such abilities, but I wasn't sure entirely what those things were specifically. I never needed to know.

Though a part of me wanted to continue tailing the shadows, I knew I had to meet up with Jax and find out what was up. Once I was high enough above the earth, I found him easily.

I joined his side and together we flew toward the cabin. Once we got close, I signaled for him to land. He nodded and followed me. Once we were on the ground we shifted back into our human forms.

"We don't have time for this," Jax said approaching me. "We have to get to the cabin to warn the others."

"Relax. We need a plan," I said. "One that doesn't involve jumping into the middle of a fight which may not have started yet."

"The plan is to get to our friends before all hell breaks out," he said. "We may already be too late."

"But we may not be," I added. "It's worth taking the few extra minutes to plan our advance. We don't want to show up and startle anyone. Especially our foes. We might inadvertently turn the tide in their favor."

He shook his head. "We don't have time to sit around and plan this out."

"We're hardly sitting," I said and leveled my gaze on him.

"Jokes. Seriously?" he asked.

"You're not thinking clearly," I said. "And the point of a joke is to avoid being serious by the way."

"My thinking is perfectly fine." He pinched the bridge of his nose and huffed. "We don't have time to stand here and argue or even form plans step by step. If you have an idea, then say it. Otherwise, I'm taking off and helping before our friends are overwhelmed."

I narrowed my eyes on him. "What are you not telling me? What do you mean before our friends are overwhelmed?"

"Bret, we have to go. Now." Jax clenched his hands into fists. "I don't have time to play twenty questions with you."

I rolled my eyes and shrugged. He desperately needed to learn how to breathe. Or find a way to alleviate his tension before it gave him a heart attack. Regardless, he was right. We didn't have all the time in the world to formulate a plan. Not that we would if we had the time. There were still too many unknowns in our approach. But I thought of one way we could make this work.

"All right, fine. As it so happens, I have an idea," I said.

"Well, let's hear it," Jax said, voice strained. "We're running out of time as it is, so make it quick."

"The way I see it is we need to gauge where they are and flank them. You take one side, and I take the other." I nodded toward him. "Does this work for you?"

"Yup. Sounds good," Jax said and looked around. "Can we go now?"

He came across as oddly nervous. It wasn't like him to behave like this. Of course, I didn't have to think about it too hard to realize his mood must have had something to do with Emily. And though she was with Marcus, she was still at ground zero. The fact didn't exactly bring comfort. Even for me.

I nodded. "Be careful. Don't lose your head in the chaos."

"Yeah. You too," he said before turning and walking away. As he moved, he shifted and took flight.

I followed suit by shifting and flying off after him.

Minutes later, we circled the cabin. I realized then what had Jax so wound up. Surrounding were hundreds upon hundreds of humans and wolves. Much more than we had anticipated, and definitely more than we would be able to handle if things ended up getting messy. We were outnumbered by a lot.

The fact we might lose someone we cared about tonight had my heart hitched into my throat. Of one thing, I was for certain, and that was I wasn't going to go down without a fight.

Since we now had an idea of the state of things, I nodded to Jax, signaling to him I had enough of a look at things. He took off to one side and disappeared, so I went to the other and landed, keeping myself in the shadows and my body close to the ground. I wasn't sure if Jax had done the same, but I stayed in my dragon form. Just in case we needed more power to fight off the band of wolves and humans than what I would provide in my human form.

Besides, it was hard to deflect lightning.

I moved in behind an unsuspecting group of humans and wolves, sticking to the shadows until the moment was right. When such a time would come to pass, I wasn't sure, but I was positive I would know it when I saw it.

For the time being, I waited.

I raked my gaze over the surrounding area. So long as I remained unseen, I just might have kept an element of surprise. The need to see what everyone was so focused on had become hard to ignore. I peeked my head through the trees. I found Emily standing in front of Marcus in his dragon form. His friends stood on the porch, unmoved by what they were watching. Well, everyone except the woman who stood off to the side. The poor thing seemed petrified.

I angled my head a little more and saw Emily's pseudo-fiancé standing in front of her with his father and another man I had no idea as to the identity of. I wasn't able to catch what they were talking about, but judging by the expression on Emily's face, she was less than moved or thrilled.

Voices started to rise. Emily's magic covered her.

Rowan charged forward and gripped both of Emily's arms into his hands. Anger boiled through my veins. That man had no business putting his hands on my woman. Lucky for me, Marcus was the man with the plan and bent his neck with his mouth opened wide, aiming to chomp the mutt's head off.

Rowan, unfortunately, jumped out of the way in the nick of time. The lucky bastard. It would have been nice if that single move had ended the fight before it got started.

I almost laughed. But I was too angry. It took everything in me not to attack right then and there.

Emily balled her fist and punched the guy full on the mouth. I smirked in the only way my snout would allow which, I was sure, would be a terrifying grin if placed on the receiving end. I was proud of her, though. She had things covered well enough, despite Marcus backing her. And that was a solid right hook she gave Rowan too.

I wanted to pat myself on the back and congratulate Jax as well. We taught her well.

Another argument ensued. I wasn't sure what it was about. Though the voices carried through the quiet night, I was too far away to discern the actual words. Even if I was able to pick out the words spoken, I truly didn't care to know what was said. I only cared about Emily and how she was literally in the middle of it all.

I hated the fact she was so close to harm. Even though Marcus stood right behind her, it wasn't enough. With the numbers surrounding the property, we were in for a bloody fight that wasn't going to end well for either side. But I was still certain we were on the losing end of things, and that meant Emily could get seriously hurt or killed.

Still, replaying the punch in my mind had me almost breathless with adoration. I couldn't help but take notice of how much had changed with her. The sweet innocence she used to have, and would throw me through a loop with, was long gone. Her eyes no longer shone with the innocence of a life without pain and suffering would show. She had scars now. Ones that were hidden deep beneath the surface.

Her years with the wolves had made her battle-hardened in a sense. Yet, throughout it all, she was still the same girl I remembered, and I had never been prouder.

Emily's hands glowed with her magic, forming balls of fire and light. She aimed both in front of her and shot the fireballs from them. They landed on the ground. Rowan screamed like a girl.

Unable to help or stop myself, I chuckled.

The sound startled the first few rows of wolves and humans standing in front of me. My chuckle had alerted the group of my presence. One by one, they turned around. The wolves growled, and the humans aimed their weapons at me.

I huffed.

They really didn't know what they were doing.

I stood up on my hind legs and flapped my wings, and then put all the force I was able to muster into slamming my feet back onto the ground. My hope was to shake the earth enough it would knock at least a couple of them off their feet. But as I touched the ground, I frowned.

They hadn't so much as shuddered.

Oh, crap, I thought seconds before the group attacked.

19

EMILY

Rowan stormed forward. I had prepared to throw magic at him, but he had advanced too quickly for that to be an option anymore. The last thing I wanted was to blow myself up. As he closed the gap between us, he wrapped his hands around my arms, squeezing them tightly. His expression twisted into one of rage. His eyes even darkened to an almost black color. "You're going to come with me, like it or not."

He tugged on me, as though I was going to obey him and let him drag me away.

"No, I'm not," I said.

"I will drag you kicking and screaming if I have to," he said.

I caught sight of Marcus bending his neck above me, mouth open wide, aimed at Rowan's head. Rowan looked up as hot breath poured over us. He screamed and jumped back, releasing my arms.

Marcus's teeth snapped together, and he lifted up with a groan, almost as though he was disappointed, he didn't get the chance to relieve Rowan of his head. I smirked at him before settling my glare on Rowan.

"Get that beast under control!" he shouted at me.

I balled up my fist and landed one on the side of his face.

The alpha's son had more than a few wires twisted in that warped brain of his. The nerve of him to put his hands on me and try to drag me from where I wanted to be. I didn't give a damn about the arrangement my family had with the wolves.

I was done.

I settled my glare on Bryson. "I suggest if you want a son after tonight, you get him under control."

Rowan growled.

"Oh, I'm sorry. Did I strike a nerve?" I asked.

Rowan's eyes narrowed on me. "I'm warning you…"

"No," I said, cutting him off. "I'm warning you to take you and your pathetic, abusive, greedy hands back to your pack and forget that you had ever met me. Or you won't have a family to go home to."

"You and what army?" he asked.

"Are we done with the pathetic lover's quarrel?" Collin asked, poking his nose into business it didn't belong getting into.

"Unless you also want a piece of this," I said, gesturing to myself, "You'll be a good little heathen and keep your mouth shut and your feet planted in that ground."

He glared at me. "How dare you!"

He and Rowan both took a step forward. Magic filled my palms. Fire as hot as my fury filled my hands. I aimed them in front of me and settled my gaze on the two men who faltered in their steps. I smirked and released my magic, launching it at the ground beneath their feet.

"You were saying?" I asked.

It was bad enough that Rowan felt the need to continuously demonstrate to me how much he could overpower me for the past couple of years. And he reminded me whenever he deemed it necessary. If I took too long bringing him tea or food… I got a beating. If I got a tone with him in the slightest, littlest bit… I got a beating. If he had a bad day… I got a beating.

Anything that didn't go exactly according to his plan, I got a demonstration on just how much bigger and stronger he was. But the beatings weren't the worst thing I had to go through. And I've delivered as many punches as he had in return.

But tonight, I had enough. This was the point where he finally got it through his head, I would never belong to him. In this life or the next. He wasn't more powerful than I was, I simply obeyed my parent's wishes and tried to make the best of the situation I was handed. He wasn't better than me. I was too amazing for him.

And though I had little idea of who this Collin character was, he was no better than Rowan.

As far as I was concerned, the two of them could go to hell together.

The men started throwing weak, pathetic insults my way. I ignored them and rolled my eyes. Then a sound erupted above the racket in front of me. The noise pulled my attention to a part of the crowd surrounding us. The humans aimed their weapons at something large. The wolves started to growl and snap their teeth in the air.

Though I wanted to finish the argument that had started in front of me, I noticed something dark moving within the trees. Black scales reflected off the light shining from the cabin.

The group attacked. Bret roared. My heart felt as though it jumped into my throat.

"Bret," I whispered.

Chaos erupted around me. Instantly, I thought of poor Cassie. She was entirely out of her element. The second I turned around, I saw her as white as a ghost while three large bears charged forward and joined the fight.

My number one priority was to get to her and help her get inside the cabin and safe and then make sure no one could get close to her. But the second I started heading in that direction, my arm was caught, and I was forced into a short spin, ending with my ex's face filling my vision.

I frowned.

I said as I struggled against him and said, "Let me go."

"No. Now you're going to listen to reason or die here with your friends," he snapped as he tried to drag me toward the woods.

I continued to struggle against him, even though he continued to tighten his hand around my arm to the point pain shot through my shoulder. "I would rather die than go anywhere with you."

I was done playing nice. I was no longer afraid of the backlash that would come from me standing my ground. Magic flooded my body. I concentrated on doing the most damage I could. This was going to hurt, and I might end up losing an arm in the process, but those were risks I was willing to take.

He brought his face closer to mine. "I will be more than happy to give that to you."

I pressed my hand into his chest. A blinding, white light exploded between us. His hand released my arm as we were thrown into the air. Seconds later, I landed with a thud on the ground. Pain ricocheted through my entire frame as I shook off the dizziness that overcame me. My arms felt weak as I struggled to climb back to my feet. But once I did, I searched the crowd for signs of Rowan.

When I blasted him, he flew into the woods somewhere. I had lost sight of him. Though I was sure he was dead, there was some room for doubt. And that meant I needed to get to Cassie before someone else did. I wouldn't be able to forgive myself if she got hurt in all this mess.

"Emily!" Cassie shouted.

I turned around, faced with someone else who stood in front of me, blocking me from getting to my friend.

I couldn't use magic so soon after the last blast. I had put so much force into it, that it would take a little while for me to use it again. The guy smirked. I glared at him.

Hand-to-hand combat it is.

He had a gun aimed at my chest. I held up my hands and took a couple steps closer.

"Stop," he said.

"Easy. You don't want to shoot me," I said.

"How do you know that, witch!" he snapped.

I smirked. "Because this isn't really your fight, now is it?"

"You're a monster. Monsters need to die," he snapped.

"I'm not a monster. I'm just like you," I said, hoping to appeal to his better judgment.

He cocked his gun. Just a couple more steps and I could take it from him. "I'm warning you… Come any closer and I will shoot!"

"No, you won't," I said and took another step. "If that was the case you would have shot me already."

I took the final step and disarmed him, taking the gun from his hand and landing a kick to his chest. He flew backward, landing on the ground and sliding a few inches. He wasn't going to die from the kick, but he would be knocked out for a little bit.

I tossed the gun to the ground and wiped my hands on my pants.

"Emily!" Cassie shrieked.

My attention snapped to her as a couple of wolves and a human approached the porch.

I quickly launched another ball of light toward the group as I rushed to her side. Her body slammed into mine. I wrapped my arms around her and guided her back into the cabin.

"It's going to be okay," I said. "Which room can you barricade into and stay safe?"

She settled her bloodshot eyes on mine. "You're not leaving me, are you?"

"I'm going to make sure you are safe first, but I have to get back out there," I said. "Now, which room?"

She nodded and made her way to one of the rooms down the hall, at the very end of the cabin. She walked in and fell onto the bed, curling up in the blanket.

I checked the window to make sure it was locked before dragging the chest of drawers over to it. I held that in place with a recliner that sat in the corner, wedging it between the chest of drawers and the bed frame.

"That should keep anyone from getting in through the window," I said, settling my attention on Cassie. "Once I leave, lock the door and don't open it unless its one of us."

She nodded. "Can't you stay with me? I would feel much safer."

I shook my head. "I wish I could, but they need me."

She sniffed and nodded. "Be careful."

I smiled gently. "I will. I promise."

Without another word, I left the room and rushed through the cabin. Once I reached the front door, I launched myself out of the cabin and off the front porch and rejoined the fight. The second my foot touched the ground, Marcus's pain-filled roar nearly made my heart stop.

20

MARCUS

The moment the collection of wolves and humans surrounding Bret started attacking him, I launched myself into the air, flapping my wings as hard as I lifted above the ground. Though I could have gone and helped him with the fight, I had confidence in Bret's ability to handle things where he was. My goal was to decrease their numbers as much as possible where I could. First, I had to get a bird's eye view of everything so I would know where I was needed.

Once I was high enough, I spotted Jax fighting another group of the hunters opposite of Bret. Jasper, Chase, and Kai busied themselves with another section, all in their bear forms. I found a place I could fit and launched myself toward our foes, landing and releasing my fire breath at the same time.

A sharp piercing pain entered my side. I let out a pain-filled roar and tried to twist to look at what had pierced my scales, but the movement was too much. From what I could gather, it was a spear bolt. An enchanted one at that. There were only so many weapons that could take out a dragon, and none of them were basic human weapons. For a bolt to be lodged in my side, it had to be enchanted.

Collin, whoever he was and wherever he had come from, had done his research. He was clever, and I wasn't going to underestimate him from here forward. But where there was one enchanted weapon designed to take out dragons, I was absolutely positive there was more, and that made me worry for my brothers. I had to trust in their ability to fight off the humans and wolves.

There was no way I was going to be able to fly. At least, not so long as I had a bolt stuck in me. I was going to have to fight from the ground. Though that was difficult enough as it was, being a massive creature confined to tight spaces with not much room to move. I didn't take into account that every breath was agony and caused the bolt to dig a little deeper. I had to figure out a way to get the thing out of me. Pronto.

Three wolves attacked, trying to rip and tear my wings, which furthered my suspicion that Collin had done his background work. I batted at two of them at first, sending them flying back into the woods. The third I picked up in my mouth and tossed over my head. Another stab of pain entered my side as the bolt dug even deeper.

I growled. Ignoring the pain, I blew out another blast of fire, desperate to get some space and time to pull the bolt out before it punctured something vital. Smoke, burning wood, and flesh filled the air. Yelps and barks echoed around me. Human screams of shock and fear joined in. But my effort was only meant to be a temporary deterrent. So long as it lasted long enough for me to figure out a way to get the spear bolt out of me, I would consider it a success.

Gritting against the pain, I stretched my neck around to my side and gripped the spear bolt in my mouth. With a deep breath in, I pulled. Blinding pain nearly downed me. My vision blurred. All I could focus on was the pain that continued to throb through me even though the bolt was removed. I spat out the piece of ammo, trying hard to stay conscious. It clamored on the ground. I stared at the object, grateful I was able to remove it.

As the seconds ticked by, the pain ebbed, my vision cleared, and my feet were steady on the ground.

I had enough time to take in a deep breath of relief before five more wolves with ten humans carrying spears surrounded me. The numbers weren't great. What was worse was I was sure the spears were enchanted, just as the bolt was. Collin, thanks to our last reaction, didn't strike me as a man who skimped on the details or the research.

The humans stared at me with mixed expressions of disgust and fury. One of the wolves growled. The humans stepped closer, stabbing me with their spears all over my body. Each pierce sent tendrils of sharp pain through my nerves, weakening me. The wolves leaped at my neck, gripping my scales in their mouths, pinching, and pulling, trying to get me to the ground.

More weight jumped on my tail and my back. More stabbing. More pain. More everything.

My heart hammered in my chest. Anxiety pulsed through my system with each beat of my heart. The chances of me making it out of this alive were growing slimmer by the second. My only hope was that Jax and Bret were fairing a lot better. Because if I didn't make it through, I needed them to take care of Emily.

I should have told them that. Before we entered into this fight. I should have mentioned it a long time ago.

No, I thought, I refused to lay down and die.

I shook the thoughts of leaving Emily, Jax, and Bret behind from my mind and took in the faces of the group that had surrounded me. I sucked in a deep breath. Fire filled my throat.

"Watch out!" a human sounded.

A spear pierced my neck. The fire died in my throat. My vision started to fade, and my heart pounded in my chest. My lungs struggled to work.

So, this really was it, I thought. This really was how I was going to die.

A single tear fell down the side of my snout as I let out a final roar. One to say goodbye. My eyes closed, and I waited for death to claim me.

A strange calm blanketed me. My body became heavy as I lay on the ground. Then a strange warmth that reminded me of a summer day surrounded me. The battle fell into a weird, dull roar and continued to decrease in volume until it whispered to me from a distance.

As the sounds of battle continued to fade away into my forgotten memories, I felt as though I was being pulled down, sinking beneath the dirt. And that sensation changed into one that was like floating on a gentle river, being carried off to whatever waited for me next.

There was no more pain. My heart was calm. I could breathe freely. Everything was peaceful. I was content to spend the rest of eternity in this place.

Echoed words I couldn't understand or even had ever heard before rushed toward me. But I didn't want to listen and didn't pay any more attention to the sound. I wanted peace. Sleep. To be carried off to my next destination.

Wherever I was, there was no pain or suffering. No worries or fears. Everything just was. And I found solace in it.

Another noise echoed toward me. My name, but it sounded distorted and strange. The voice was familiar and pulled at me. It belonged to a woman. She sounded upset and worried. Not at all how I would imagine someone calling me to the afterlife. Memories flipped through my mind, trying to fit the voice to a person in my past.

The pull stopped. The peacefulness around me started to fade away. I didn't want to let it go, but I didn't have a choice. I was forced in the direction of the sound.

Pain encompassed me. The heat of a nearby fire kissed my skin.

No. Something wasn't right. What I felt wasn't right.

"Marcus!" the woman said. "Get up!"

"Emily?" I tried to call out, but my voice had failed me. I only thought her name.

"We have to move, get up now!" Emily said. Her voice was much clearer.

She was close. So very close. All I had to do was reach out and touch her. But I couldn't get my body to move. It rebelled against me, ignoring every command I gave it.

"Open your eyes," she said, closer than ever. I could almost feel her breath on my face.

Something struck my cheek. "Get up!"

My eyes peeled open instantly, and I saw the night sky above. Just to my right, Emily sat next to me on her hands and knees. A ring of fire surrounded us.

"Oh, thank God. You have to get up," she said. "I'm losing control of the ring."

I fought against my protesting muscles and sat up.

"There you go," she said, coaxing me. "Keep going."

"How did you?" I started to ask.

"Now isn't the time," she said. "I can't hold this for much longer. Can you fight?"

"I think so," I said.

"Can you shift?" she asked.

I shook my head. "I don't know. Probably not."

"Well, then grab a gun from the over by the porch and let's get moving," she said.

I gaped at her. I couldn't believe that she was taking charge in the way she was. Then again, she was a natural at almost everything else she had done.

"Marcus, go!" she commanded and dropped the ring of fire.

I nodded and carefully jogged toward the porch where a collection of different firearms was cast aside. I picked up a couple of them and frowned. I hated violence. I hated taking lives. That's why I became a doctor. To save lives and encourage health. But this was a war and killing was regrettably unavoidable.

And considering I refused to let another shifter fall at the hands of a crazed psychopath, killing was also necessary.

I checked the clips and pulled back on the barrel to load a bullet in each pistol. Wolves charged forward, running around Emily who was busy taking out the humans with the spears. I aimed and fired as a wolf leaped to my back, forcing me forward. As I landed on the ground, dirt entered my mouth. The pistols flew from my hands. My body ached from the jarring collision with the ground. I glanced up as two wolves picked them up in their snouts and ran into the woods.

"No!" I screamed. The last thing they needed was a collection of weapons. We needed to disarm the attackers, not make it easier for them to defend themselves.

Humans rushed toward me, stopping as their fear-filled gazes took in something from behind me.

Growls from larger animals than the wolves approached my side, stopping the humans from reaching me. And just in the nick of time. A few more feet, and they would have been on me.

I spat out the dirt and pushed myself up to my knees. A bear stood on either side of me and leaned into me to help me up from the ground. By the looks of them, it was Kai and Jasper. I nodded in thanks, then they rushed out to help with the fight that had moved into the front yard.

Surprisingly, it appeared like things were going a lot better than I thought.

2 1

EMILY

I had sucked in a breath and had held it for so long I almost forgot to keep breathing. Everything around me slowed to almost a standstill, as I watched Marcus collapse onto the ground. For a brief pause, everything inside me stopped working. I knew I had to get to him. To help save him from the assholes stabbing him with spears. But I couldn't get over the initial shock of him falling to the ground. It nearly killed me watching him lay on the ground. After a few beats, I forced myself to move my feet and get to his side.

Then his dragon faded into his human form, and I knew he was in serious trouble. When I finally made it to him, my legs gave out and I fell to my knees at his side. He looked so pale, and he was covered in bruises. Blood soaked his clothes. I couldn't tell if he was breathing.

My heart broke. Tears filled my eyes and raced down my cheeks.

Vague shapes moved around me, but I didn't care about them. Marcus was dying, and there was nothing I could do about it.

Grief filled me while I stared at his still form, and then something inside me other than despair brewed. It was such a strange sensation. My grief had overpowered me, but this something… this other thing I couldn't put my finger on, it was so much stronger. Whatever it was, it brought with it a hefty dose of rage.

That sensation had filled me to the brim. When I couldn't hold it back anymore, I held out my hands to the side and screamed into the night air. My hands formed fists and I slammed them into the ground. Fire erupted from the dirt, launching three feet into the air, surrounding us in a perfect ring.

I cried as the fires continued to snap and burn. The group that had taken Marcus down, backed away cautiously as they watched with a collection of shocked and frightened expressions. I didn't care. I was too hurt and overcome with the fact I was losing someone I loved. They were lucky I wasn't snuffing out each of their lives.

Marcus gasped. I sucked in a breath of shock as hope washed over me.

As I maintained the ring of fire surrounding us, I started trying to wake him up.

"Marcus!" My voice came out high-pitched and full of worry.

He didn't move. Or respond. He only continued to lie on the ground.

As I continued to call out for him, he slowly started to stir. He wasn't lost to me yet, which was a huge relief. But the more effort I put into waking him up, the less concentration I was giving to the ring. And if the ring of fire fell, the humans and wolves would attack again, and I would lose Marcus for sure.

There had to be a way for me to get him up and moving much quicker than screaming at him.

Then I slapped him. His eyes peeled open, and he rolled to his back, wincing in pain. At least he woke up. I was losing control over the ring of fire that erupted. I could feel the magic within me fading. I couldn't protect him forever.

He needed to move.

And when he did, Cassie's scream filtered from inside the cabin. I sucked in a breath, dropped the ring, and rushed toward the cabin door. The second I stepped inside, I caught three men standing in the hallway, just outside the door Cassie had barricaded herself behind. They banged on the door and threw themselves against it. The door vibrated against their movements, but it wouldn't be long before it gave away completely. Before it did, I had to do something to stop them.

"Hey!" I shouted, drawing their attention.

One of them turned out to be a woman with a military buzz and deep green eyes. She smiled. "I'll let you boys handle this one. I'll take care of the girl."

"I wouldn't do that if I were you," I warned.

One of her lackeys, a skinny blond with crooked teeth, said, "Or you'll what? Hex me?"

His partner, a chunky guy with no eyebrows, laughed so hard his round belly shook. "So terrifying."

I pretended to check my nails and sucked on my teeth before settling my gaze back on them. "Nah. I wouldn't want to break a nail."

"That's not the only thing that's going to break on you," blondie said.

"Filthy witch," the fat one said. "You should have left well enough alone."

"Oh, you do know how to speak," I said. "Here I thought you were as dumb as you looked."

"That's not very nice," he said, playing up a pout.

"Awe…" I said, playing up the sarcasm. "I hurt the poor man's feelings."

He smiled and cracked his knuckles on his palms. "Now I'm gonna have to teach you a lesson in respect."

I laughed and then squared my legs, dipping into my ready stance. "Oh, that was a good one. You got any others?"

The two men charged. The skinny one got to me first and tried to land a punch to my gut. I grabbed his wrist with one hand, turned my back toward his torso, and rammed him in the nose with the elbow of my free arm. Blondie jerked back, moaning as he covered his nose.

The fat man tried to grab me, and I out the way, spinning to face him head-on and kicking him in his precious jewels. He bowled over. I rammed my knee into his face. With both men holding their noses with blood oozing from around their fingers, I faced the woman who continued to try and break down Cassie's door.

"Your turn," I said.

She ignored me.

I approached her and cleared my throat. She ignored me again.

I was angry before, but now I was furious and gripped her shoulder, digging my fingers underneath her collar bone. She nearly collapsed to her knees, crying out in pain.

"Let go, dammit!" she said.

"Next time, I suggest you listen when I try to get your attention. Didn't your mother tell you it was rude to ignore people?"

"Must have missed that day in class," she snapped, prying at my fingers to release her.

I nodded. "Oh, you got jokes too. Must be a thing. I'm jealous."

She spat in my face. "Laugh at that, bitch."

I wiped my face free of her spit then punched her in her temple. Her face was knocked into the wall. She groaned as she shook off the dizziness that surely filled her head. Then she slowly glared at me.

I smirked at her. "Challenge accepted."

She stood and swung her fists at me, one at a time, chasing me down the hallway. Each one I managed to avoid. Frustrated, she stopped at the end of the hall and growled.

"Hold still!" she demanded.

I shook my head. "Nope. Gonna play hard to get. It's more fun this way."

With rage in her eyes, she charged me. I twisted out of the way. She stopped in the middle of the room and took one look at her friends before settling her death glare on me. "You're going to pay for that."

"Funny how that keeps getting said to me and I have yet to pay for anything," I muttered.

She charged. This time, I held still. When she got close enough, I punched her in the gut, gripped her by her shoulders, and dipped low, pulling her over my head. As I climbed back to my feet, she faced me. I kicked her in her stomach, sending her flying down the hall. She collapsed onto the floor. I stood and turned around. The skinny blond had recovered. The fat guy was still rolling on the ground holding his nuts with one hand and his nose with the other. I shook my head.

"Men are such babies," I muttered.

"You're gonna pay for that," the skinny blond dude said.

I rolled my eyes and shrugged. "Original. You people really need to broaden your vocabulary. And I might pay for what I've done, but you're hardly going to be the one to collect."

He pressed his lips together and charged. I jumped into the air and angled myself slightly to the side and brought my knees up to my chest. As he came closer, I pushed my feet out, landing both of them square in his chest. The skinny guy learned what it meant to fly for a few seconds before crashing into the wall next to the door. He fell to the floor in a lump.

I looked at the fat guy who stared at me with a death glare.

"What are you gonna do next?" I asked, standing my ground.

He rolled his eyes and shook his head.

"Yeah, I thought so," I said.

He got the point, and so did the other two, but there was no way I was going to leave this cabin with them inside it.

"Bitch," the fat one said.

"Well unless you want a second lesson in how much of a bitch I can be, I suggest you take yourself out the door and pronto."

He stared at me for a few seconds, seemingly mulling over his options.

"Do I need to count?" I asked.

He shook his head, huffed, and managed to get to his feet before stepping out the door. I nodded to myself and turned around. I grabbed the chick by the collar and pulled her along the floor toward the front door. Once she was out, I got her to the stairs and dropped her. Next was the blond guy, and I was thankful he was already close to the door.

I went back inside long enough to knock on the door that sealed Cassie in.

"Go away!" she shouted.

"It's me," I said. "Are you all right?"

"Yeah, I'm fine. Just terrified. How is everything out there?" she asked through the door. Her voice came through clearer and louder, letting me know that she stood right inside the door.

"Still up in the air," I said. "Sit tight."

"How are my men?" she asked.

I smiled. "Handling themselves quite well."

I honestly wasn't sure. But if they were anything like mine, they were dealing more damage than they took.

"Be careful," she said.

"Always," I said and headed back outside and into the fight.

Part of the forest was on fire. Thankfully, it stayed well contained. The last thing we needed was the forest going up in flames. But the smell of burning flesh and wood had filled the air, carried on a breeze that blew in gusts.

I really hoped the fire wouldn't spread.

A howl ripped through the air and all the wolves instantly turned their tails and ran.

"Fucking cowards," I muttered. Though it really didn't shock me. Bryson had done a banging job of demonstrating his talent for leaving at the most inopportune moment. I wondered if he found Rowan and decided he had suffered enough loss for one lifetime.

Regardless, the wolves retreated into the woods.

Another terrifying roar tore through the air, stilling my heart and my lungs. I searched for Marcus, finding him clutching his side, meeting my gaze. He nodded once and looked in the direction of where the sound came from.

With my heart racing, I rushed toward the spot he indicated.

I hated the idea of one of my men being severely hurt. And I hoped with everything in me I could make it to him before it was too late. And I prayed to any deity that would listen to me that I wasn't.

2 2
JAX

I wanted to rush to Bret. More so to snap at him for not waiting for the signal than to save him from his mistake. I should have known he would do something to mess things up. He couldn't follow directions to save his soul. But before I could take a single step in his direction, the wolves and humans standing in front of me had looked toward the direction of the commotion, and found me.

I groaned and stretched my neck as far as I could to make myself look more menacing. Sadly, it didn't work.

The wolves and humans lunged at me. Chaos erupted around the cabin.

Taking on an army of wolves and humans with enchanted weapons wasn't my idea of a good time. Then again, there had been a lot of not-so-good times as of late. But this one was the worst. Especially since we were all separated, and the enemy had gotten the drop on us instead of the other way around.

As the saying went, the best plans always went astray. Except for this situation, it wasn't a "suck it up and deal with it" scenario. This one had deadly consequences.

My foes came at me by the handfuls. But I wasn't going to let them intimidate me. If they wanted to attack first. Fine. So be it. But they were going to find out exactly who they were dealing with.

I lowered myself to the ground, angled my head, and let out a deep, rumbling growl. Frost billowed from my snout. It was a warning to them what they were getting if they insisted on taking on an ice dragon.

They didn't so much as flinch. Instead, they attacked me by the handfuls. Each round, the number of humans and wolves was different. And every time I took a few out with my claws, some with my tail, and others with my teeth. Somehow, they managed to get me just as much as I got them. I couldn't tell how my brothers and Emily were doing from this angle, but I had a bad feeling it wasn't much better than I was.

Especially for Marcus. I knew his roar anywhere, and it had sounded pained. My heart raced with the sound as worry for my friend and brother took my attention from the fight in front of me. I didn't have time to break away and run to his aid, no matter how much I wanted to. Because it occurred to me that the army of wolves and humans had one particular goal in common for this fight. And the goal was separating us.

Well, it worked.

Six shifters and a witch, fighting side by side was more than even these numbers could handle. But barely. We would have had this war done shortly after it started. But we all had played right into their hands. And we were paying the price for such a dire mistake.

Likely with our lives.

But I wasn't going to go down so easily. It was going to take a whole lot more than a few bumps and scrapes to take me out.

The latest of the waves was a group of four wolves and one human. The human held a weapon in his hand. A hunting knife if I saw correctly. I snorted at him. He could do some serious damage with that blade, but I wasn't going to show him a lick of fear. He was beneath me. I was more powerful than he could ever hope to be, and his courage was only because he held a weapon that could actually cut through my scales. I was willing to be he didn't have an iota of an idea enchanted weapons existed to take out dragons before joining this army of idiots.

Once I took care of this latest wave of attackers, I might be able to gain the upper hand. From there, I my goal was to increase the momentum and take out as many of their numbers as possible.

Then a howl cut through the air, signaling a retreat. The wolves turned tail and ran.

"Don't you dare stop fighting!" Collin screamed. "The wolves were cowards!"

Oh good, I thought. He was exactly what we needed to deal with. A maniac leading a band of humans who had knowledge they shouldn't have.

I growled in response to the sound of man's voice, but the humans in front of me hesitated. They had a variety of weapons that I was sure would prove interesting if they tried to hit me with them. It didn't seem possible for all of them to be enchanted. In the least, figuring out which ones weren't enchanted would be somewhat entertaining.

Painful, but entertaining.

Nevertheless, I faced the humans and sucked in a deep breath. Ice filled my throat as I prepared to launch my magic onto my foes. I wondered if human popsicles were in Collin's great and terrible plan.

Probably not.

Still, I sought out the challenge and exhaled frost.

The humans ducked and dodged my attacks. Some ran away. The ones that didn't, stood by and waited for their moment to attack. I didn't want to follow them in every direction they went because I needed to be careful of where my ice magic hit. I wasn't sure where my comrades were, and I didn't want to accidentally freeze one of my friends or Emily.

I would never be able to forgive myself for that if she had gotten hurt because of me.

Footsteps pounded the ground, collecting around me. Instantly, sharp piercing pain entered my body in all directions. My wing was torn. I groaned out and swiped with my talons, hoping to decrease the amount of pain that entered my system.

But it was no use.

I couldn't fly. I couldn't use my magic. I could barely even think straight.

Burning fire entered my other wing. I flapped it and quickly glanced at what was left of my poor, tattered wing. These people wanted to disable me completely before killing me.

That was just cruel.

But a strange sensation started to take hold. My heart started to race, and my lungs didn't want to work. Panic filled me. I started lashing out because I knew it wouldn't be long before I was a goner. And I was going to fight to my last breath. Enchanted weapons or not, I wasn't going to make taking me out easy on them.

Sharp pain entered my side. Blinding, searing pain burned through me. Something wet and sticky poured over my scales. Whatever weapon they used on me had wounded me pretty bad. Really, bad.

The humans wouldn't let up. I started to lose my grip on reality, and my consciousness started to fade. I blinked my eyes and shook my head as I continued to fight tooth and nail to make it through.

But the sad state of affairs? I was becoming weaker by the second, and I might as well have been trying to tickle them versus slapping the life out of them.

As the black rim surrounding my vision started to grow, it occurred to me the humans had done extensive research of our kind to be able to take out two of us. So far, the only one I hadn't heard was Bret. But... and this was a big but, there was a possibility that he didn't have enough time to roar.

I hoped he was okay. A world without my brothers would be a harder, much colder world to live in.

But it didn't change the fact that our enemies had done enough research to know exactly how to disarm and disable a dragon to kill it. With the evidence to support my theory, things didn't bode well for me and my team. But I found peace in joining Marcus on the other side... that was if he had died.

If not, I hope he was giving the remaining people still fighting hell. Lots of it.

Things were looking grim. My resolve to stay up on my feet was slipping. I was losing consciousness by the second. I let out a long and painful roar. I didn't want to die, but if I had to in order for others, especially shifters, to live… In that case, my death would be a good one. I couldn't think of a better reason to die.

Just as my vision started to fade, Emily's blurred form jumped in front of me.

I tried to step forward, to get her out of harm's way, but I stumbled and nearly bumped into her. My heart pounded harder. She shouldn't have come. I couldn't stand the thought of her standing in the way of the ones trying to kill me. She was going to get herself hurt.

I wanted to fight against my failing body and keep her safe. I would gladly give my life to make sure she lived. I tried to take another step forward and dizziness overwhelmed me.

Fear worked its way through my system as the terrifying fact echoed through my mind. I was dying, and she had put herself between me and my killers.

I tried to blink away the dark rim that was taking more and more of my vision by the second, but it seemed to have done me no use. Just when I would get my vision in focus, it would blur again.

Then I watched as her form moved and held what breath I had left. She faced the humans and lifted up her hands. A bright light grew from her fists, swallowing everything in sight, and stole away her image. As the light faded, so did all the sounds around me.

A distinct sensation of falling blanketed me as darkness fell all around me. I exhaled the breath from my lungs and surrendered to the dark.

23
EMILY

I didn't know what had come over me. But whatever it was that I had done, it incinerated the humans trying to kill Jax. That was the final straw for the human army. Despite all of Collin's demands and threats, every last remaining member of his army left him. With nowhere else to turn to, he sulked into the shadows.

"This isn't over. I'll be back, and when I do, I'll erase shifters from the world," he said as he faded into the trees.

After ensuring the bear shifters had things covered and Cassie was doing fine, Marcus carried me back to the castle. Bret carried Jax's human form. He had lost a lot of blood, and there was no telling whether or not he was going to make it.

Bret had surprisingly come out of the battle with little more than scratches and bruises. Apparently, no one took him seriously. Or maybe it was the fact that he blended so well into the shadows that he used them to his advantage.

Whatever the reason, I was grateful he was okay. And Marcus too.

A couple of hours after the fight was over, we were back at the castle, and Marcus was hard at work, trying to save Jax's life. The few hours I had spent waiting in silence with Bret were the longest I had ever had to endure in my life.

"I should probably go back and help clean up and make sure all the fires don't become bigger ones," Bret said after a while.

"You're seriously leaving?" I asked, shocked.

He smirked at me, but it was full of sadness. "Jax is my brother, and I don't do so well with bad news. It's probably best that I keep myself busy."

I stood up with him and walked him to the door. "Please be careful."

He smiled. "Psshh, I got this."

I smiled too, but the humor at the moment was short-lived. And once Bret was gone, I was alone, and the silence was overbearing. I didn't have anything to keep me busy. I was too sore to train, too tired to clean, and I didn't have the energy to take a bath or shower.

So, instead, I headed to the infirmary. Well, what worked as a makeshift one anyway. I took a seat on the floor and clutched my head in my hands. Of all the people to lose in the fight, it looked like it had to be him.

Though I knew Marcus was doing everything he could to save Jax, and then some, it brought little comfort. He was in bad shape when I found him. Too much blood had covered him and the ground. The humans were celebrating Jax's demise as though he was already dead.

Tears burned my eyes as I waited, and waited, and waited. What seemed like hours later, Marcus finally came out of the room. He sighed, wiping his hands dry with a paper towel. His eyes fell to mine and there was enormous sadness in them.

"I've done everything I could," Marcus said. "It's up to him now."

I nodded. "Thank you."

"You can go in and sit with him. He'll be out for at least a couple more hours… and that's if he even wakes up."

I swatted at a couple of tears that fell down my cheek. Marcus cupped my cheek and brushed away the trail left behind with his thumb. "Whatever happens, I'll be here for you."

I nodded. "Thank you again."

"Don't thank me yet," he said. "Thank me when this is all over."

"Okay," I whispered.

He removed his hand and shuffled his feet down the hallway toward his room. The door's mechanism clicked open. Seconds later, the door shut, leaving an unsettling silence.

With a sigh, I poked my head into the room. Jax laid on the bed, as still as could be. Tears flooded my eyes as I slowly crossed the room to his bedside. He was pale from the loss of blood. And his breathing was too shallow for comfort.

I never wanted to be as close to him as I did watching him cling to life by a thread. The last thing I wanted was for him to leave the world without me by his side.

So, I carefully climbed into bed next to him. I rested my head on his shoulder and listened to his breathing. I was too terrified to sleep and clung to every second I could with him. And as the minutes ticked by, his breathing slowly deepened, bringing with it a rush of relief.

He was going to be okay.

Minutes later, his arm moved and wrapped around me. He sucked in a deep breath and then winced.

"Don't do that, it hurts," I said softly.

He snorted. "I've been through worse."

We lay in silence. This time it wasn't uncomfortable. Without warning, Jax rolled over me, looked me deep in the eyes, and said, "I should have done this a long time ago."

He kissed me. But not like he did in the kitchen. In the way that said so much more than his words ever could. His hands started to remove my clothing. I grabbed his hand to stop him.

He leaned up and stared at me with a confused expression.

"You almost died, and now you want to have sex?" I asked.

He smiled. "Babe, it would take a whole lot more to take me out."

I tried to argue but he placed a finger over my lips and shushed me.

I glared at him.

"Just go with it," he whispered.

I rolled my eyes, but I couldn't deny my heightened arousal even if I tried. I knew better than to think he didn't already sense it. That was probably part of what had egged him on.

He smirked kissed me again while my shirt was hiked up over my breasts. His mouth left mine long enough for my shirt to be pulled off entirely, then he went for my pants. He winced.

"Told you," I said.

He huffed at me. "A little help?"

I sighed even though my lips had stretched into a smile. "Okay."

I took off my pants and panties, all in one motion, and then joined him under the covers. He curled in next to me, pulling me close to him.

"That's more like it," he murmured.

I chuckled. "Just don't get overzealous and injure yourself more."

"I make no promises," he said. Before I had a chance to argue, he kissed me again while climbing over me. I spread my legs to allow him better access to my sex. He laid over me, his erection pressing against me in the most delightful way.

Against my lips, he said, "I've wanted to do this with you for a long time."

"Really?" I asked.

He nodded then situated the tip of his dick at my entrance and slowly pressed into me. I sucked in a breath as warmth washed over me. I exhaled in a sigh.

"We're just getting started," he said as he pushed himself inside me a little more.

With each push inside me, he filled me more and more until he was fully inside me and still had some room to go. It was hard to believe the length he had on him. I probably wouldn't have believed it if I wasn't witnessing and experiencing it myself.

I spread my legs wider, hooking them around his waist to allow him full access to my sex. He entered the rest of the way and then situated himself. He tucked his arms under mine, gripping my shoulders with his hands.

With slow movements, he pushed into me, grinding his hips against mine, and brushing along my clit. I wrapped my arms around him, digging the tips of my fingers into his skin as he slid deeper and deeper into me.

Jax buried his head into the crook of my neck. His breaths deepened and with each exhale, warm air covered my skin. Every once in a while, he would leave a kiss on my neck or at the base of my ear.

My orgasm started to build in a slow, delicate way. The whole time it felt relaxed and sensual. For such a serious guy, he knew how to take his time and really enjoy the moment with me. His movements were concentrated for my pleasure, which I also appreciated.

And in moments when he was getting too close to his release, he slowed down to kiss me. During one of these times, he pulled out of me as he planted kisses along my chest, stopping at each breast, sucking and massaging them.

Once he was done, he lifted up to settle his gaze on me and smirked. "How do you best like to be pleased?"

"That's a first," I said, shocked.

His eyebrows drew together. "No one has ever asked you what you liked before?"

I shook my head. "Is that weird?"

"How else is a man to know how to please his woman?" he asked.

"I'm your woman now?" I asked.

"Partner, lover, fling… semantics," he said.

"I loved everything you have done so far. But I also like to be touched and I'm fond of Cunnilingus."

His eyes darkened and his mouth parted slightly. "In that case, lay back and enjoy what I'm about to do to you."

"Okay," I said as he shifted downward between my legs. His mouth kissed the top of my delicate mound, causing a chill to ripple through me.

Fingers slid inside my entrance as his tongue flicked my clit. I sucked in a shuddering breath and my eyes rolled closed. His mouth continued to dance along my sensitive nub while his fingers dug inside me.

Pressure built between my hips and I fought against the urge to wiggle my hips or allow my thighs to close on his head.

Within a few short, delicious minutes, my orgasm hit. It was hard not to scream. His movements slowed to drag out the climax for as long as he could. And when it finally settled, he kissed his way back up to my mouth for a short peck.

"How was that?" he asked.

"Amazing," I breathed out.

"Okay. Now I want to try something," he said. "Roll to your side."

I did so, smiling.

Jax situated himself behind me and lifted up my leg, draping it over his hips. His erection rested against my entrance. As he guided his cock inside my wet pussy, I gripped the sheet covering the bed. He gently slid his leg between mine and as he moved, his thigh caressed my clit, edging me closer to another climax.

All the while, his hands explored every inch of my body that he could reach.

After a few moments, I shuddered, clutched the bedding into my fists, and sighed.

"Oh, come on," he said. "You can do better than that."

He pulled out of me and climbed back over me, slamming into my sex. I gasped.

"Like this?" he asked.

I nodded.

He sat on his knees and draped my legs over his shoulders, then he leaned over me in a plank position and pumped into me. His dick hit my g-spot and it became hard to breathe and focus on anything else except for the sensations rushing through my body.

I clung to his arms as I cried out through another wave of pleasure, and once it ended, I pushed him off me and climbed to my knees. "I also like it like this… but not gently."

"Damn, I love a woman who knows what she likes and isn't afraid to say it," he said as he positioned himself at my entrance.

He placed his hands on my hips and shoved himself into me. The forcefulness made me angle my hips toward him and lower my chest to the bed. With each slam into me came a clap from our skin colliding together.

It didn't take long for another orgasm to hit.

He pulled out of me and laid on the bed. "Ride me."

I smirked. "Are you sure you could handle it?"

He gazed at me with a smile. "I wouldn't have told you to if I couldn't."

"Fair point," I said and straddled him.

I hovered above the tip of his dick, teasing him with my entrance by wiggling my hips into a circle, almost belly dancing on top of him.

His fingers wrapped around my hips, and I slowly slid him inside me. Once I was situated, I rocked back and forth, moving in slow circles, grinding my sex against his body.

His hands moved to my ass and squeezed as his head pushed deeper into the mattress. He stiffed, and his dick throbbed.

"I'm getting close," he said.

I smiled and kept the momentum going. The second he started to orgasm, he took control. I leaned forward as he hammered into me. Hot liquid spilled into me, and my own climax hit. He kept moving until it faded, making me appreciate him as a lover all the more.

Once his movements ceased, I continued to lay on his chest, listening to the sound of his heart racing. His breathing slowly returned to normal. Once his dick slid out of me, I shimmied to his side and nestled into the crook of his shoulders.

Jax placed a kiss on my forehead as my eyes started to close.

"Stay with me," he said.

"I am," I whispered back.

I fell into a deep sleep.

24

BRET

One week after the battle that nearly tore my brothers apart and destroyed Emily, I returned home from a patrol shift. I was sent out to search for any stragglers left in the woods and to do a little recon on the wolves to see if they were preparing to make another appearance or unexpected visit.

So far, everything checked out... for now.

There was no telling when the wolves would rear their ugly heads again. I was sure they would eventually, but for now, it was nice to enjoy the peace. As for the humans? No one could figure out where they came from or where they went. But I had a sinking suspicion it was only a matter of time before we saw Collin again too.

Once I stepped inside the castle, I searched for Marcus, though I had a feeling I knew where he would be. A few, short minutes later, I found him stewing on his balcony. Exactly where I thought he would be. He looked at the sky, watching as the sun poked through the thick clouds that typically hovered above us. I quietly joined his side and looked out over the valley.

I loved the view. I loved the land. I even loved the sky. The area was normally a quiet little spot of paradise. Despite the recent battle, the view still helped me feel calm and centered.

"Hey," I said.

"Hey," Marcus said in return.

I searched his face. There was a hint of worry that pulled at the corners of his mouth. His eyes seemed heavy. I could almost hear the gears turning in his head.

"What's wrong?" I asked.

"How did it go?" Marcus asked, ignoring my question.

His voice sounded as though he was lost in thought, which was what I figured he was doing. This was his thinking spot. It was also his favorite place in the castle, but if there was a problem to work out, he would always do it on the balcony. Most of the time alone. I had no idea what it was about this place, but it worked. Maybe it was the view. The calming effect it had on me and Marcus. I never thought to ask Jax about it. Though I had a feeling it would be the same for him too.

"All clear for now," I said. "There are no signs of human camps. They've all cleared out."

He nodded. "We'll keep doing rotations. They'll be back eventually. The only question is when."

"Agreed," I said. "So are you going to answer my question now?"

He glanced at me with a confused expression.

I shook my head. "What's eating you?"

He huffed and his head drooped a little. "I can't stop thinking about Emily."

"What about her?" I asked, trying to ignore the spike of panic that set my heart racing. "Did something happen?"

"No. Nothing happened. I just…" He twisted to face me. "Well, you are already aware of how much I missed her when she left the last time."

I nodded. "I didn't think you would ever recover."

"To be honest," he said as he returned his gaze over the valley, "I wasn't so sure myself."

"So… is she leaving?" I asked, still trying not to sound too worried.

He shook his head. "I'm not sure. I can't bring myself to let her go if she wanted to."

"Why would she be going somewhere?" I asked.

He shook his head. "I don't know. She said from the beginning her staying here was only temporary."

I nodded, processing the information he had just given me. It was true what he said. Emily made it clear her staying in the castle was a temporary arrangement. But like him, I couldn't stand the thought of her leaving. And the thought that she would, now that things were settling down, made my heart sink.

"I love her too," I said through a heavy sigh.

Marcus nodded. "Believe me, I'm well aware of that. As much as the fact bothers me."

"What do you propose we do?" I asked. "We can't very well force her to stay. That would only blow up in our faces."

"Force who to stay?" Jax asked, pulling my attention to him. He leaned against the doorway to the balcony with his arms crossed over his chest and his legs at the ankles. He smiled.

"Well look at who's up and about and looking as fresh as a dragon back from the dead can be," I said, turning around and resting against the wall of the balcony.

"Almost one hundred percent," he said, joining us. He stood on the other side of Marcus. "You can't get rid of me that easily."

"The fact that you are doing so well is a miracle in and of itself," Marcus added. "What about your dragon?"

Jax shook his head. The frown on his face said everything. "Still working on that."

Marcus clapped the man on the shoulder. "Give him time. He'll come around when he's ready."

"I hope so," Jax said. "Now, about the topic I stumbled in on..."

"Emily," I offered. "Who else would we be talking about."

"I figured as much," he said. "I take it she's leaving?"

"We don't know," Marcus said. "But the going consensus is we don't want her to go."

"She can't leave," Jax said. "I'll talk to her. Reason with her to stay."

"None of us want to see her go," I said. "But pushing her up against a corner isn't going to do us any favors."

"What can we do to make her stay though?" Marcus added.

"Why don't we just ask her?" Jax asked.

"We could," Marcus said, returning to his thoughts. "How is the question. It needs to be special."

"Wait," I said, holding up my hand. "Are you saying what I think you're saying?"

He sighed. "Sharing her is far better than a life lived without her."

"Yeah, but…" Jax said. "Would she accept the three of us? I mean it's one thing to be casual but there's a whole other thing when you consider a relationship with three different men, no matter how close we all are."

"And we could do far worse than sharing one woman," I said. "Besides, we're brothers. We've shared many things."

"A woman, especially one like Emily, is a bit different than the things we've shared in the past," Marcus said. "She's not an object or a meal."

"Speak for yourself," I said and chuckled when Marcus glared at me.

"He's got a point there," Jax said.

"I get that, but would it really be that bad?" I asked.

Jax and Marcus shrugged.

"I, personally, think it would be the best thing ever," I said.

Marcus and Jax glanced at me with a mix of expressions from confusion and questioning my sanity.

"My point is, if we want Emily to stay, we have to be willing to share her. Pushing her against a wall or even trying to make her decide which one of us to be with will likely end up badly for everyone involved. So, before we go any further on this, we have to all agree that we won't fight over her."

Silence settled on us as I waited for Jax and Marcus's response. After several minutes I sighed.

"Someone please tell me we're all in agreeance," I said.

Jax raised his hand. "I can't lose her. I would do whatever it took to keep her happy, even if that is sharing her."

"I already told you my thoughts," Marcus said. "Please don't make me repeat myself."

I nodded. "Then we have this settled."

"Not yet, it isn't," Marcus said. "We still have to find out if Emily is willing to be with the three of us."

"She will," I said. "I have a feeling she will."

"We could do a special dinner for her," Jax offered. "Candlelight, dessert, wine, the works."

Marcus nodded.

"I like where you're going with this," I said. "But how is that going to help us with figuring out if she would accept us or not?"

"There's only one way to find out," Jax said and looked to Marcus.

He sighed. "Dinner. We'll give her the rest of the day to rest up and relax, then at dinner, we'll ask her."

"All right, we got a plan," I said. "Now all we have to do is execute. I'll go shopping."

"I will do the cooking," Jax said.

"I guess I'll run the bath," Marcus said. At least this time he sounded more hopeful and was a bit more lively.

"We're going to need to clean up too," I said.

"One step at a time," Marcus said, holding up his hand. "Go to the store. Jax and I will handle things here until you come back."

I nodded. "Yes, sir."

Without another word, I turned around and headed back out of the castle. I had little doubts things wouldn't pan out for us... but I still couldn't shake the nervousness that worked its way through me.

I hated the thought of a life without Emily. And in the off chance that she wouldn't accept the three of us, I would probably shrivel up and die. Or my heart would at the very least.

EMILY

I was sitting in the living room, watching tv when Marcus came in and held out his hand.

I smiled at him. "What?"

Wordlessly, he stared at me. There was a certain glint in his eyes that tugged on the corners of his lips in the smallest, almost undetectable way. I bit my lip as my eyes trailed along his body. Bits of the night we shared flashed through my mind.

I slid my hand on top of his. His fingers wrapped around my palm. He tugged, pulling me from the couch, and then led me through the castle to my bedroom, where the sound of rushing water filled the air. I sucked in a deep breath and sighed. The aroma was rose and lavender.

"Are you not going to tell me what this is all about?" I asked.

"You'll see," he said.

"Uh-huh," I said as we entered my bedroom. "A bubble bath is hardly a surprise."

I was trying to bait him into telling me what he was up to. He only smirked, letting me know that not only did my attempt fall flat, it also humored him.

"Who said anything about a surprise?" he asked. He guided me to the bathroom and shut off the water filling the tub before he turned and faced me. He stared at me patiently.

I quirked an eyebrow. "You're not expecting to undress me too, are you?"

He chuckled. "No, but I do want to help you into the bath."

"Uh… okay…" I said.

Marcus was acting especially weird. He had never behaved like this before. So, my suspicions were raised as to what exactly was going on. But I know I couldn't ask him again. He had already shut down the last time I asked. I still wanted to figure out what was going on though.

I got undressed. Right down to my birthday suit.

His eyes widened and took in the length of my body, clearly admiring what he saw. I propped a hand on my hip, stared him deep into his eyes, and asked, "What is all this about?"

He smiled. "Do I have to have a reason to do nice things for you?"

I shrugged. "I suppose not. But this is rather random and sudden."

"So?" he asked.

"Since when are you random?" I asked, keeping my eyes locked on his.

He held out his hand. "Just get in and enjoy the bath, would you?"

I knew better than to think his statement was a question, and I had to admit that the bath looked extremely inviting. After a few more seconds spent on deciding whether to push the issue or not, I gave up and held out my hand for Marcus to take.

The warmth of his skin filled mine and he helped me into the bath. The second my foot touched the hot water set at the perfect temperature, goosebumps prickled along my skin. I lowered my body into the water and leaned back with a sigh as my eyes rolled closed.

The sensations were absolute heaven.

"Take your time," Marcus said. "I'll be back in an hour to help you out."

I waved him off. "Make it two."

The bath was exactly what the doctor ordered. No pun intended.

And I was going to stay in the water until everything from the past couple of weeks melted away.

* * *

LATER ON, in the evening, long after the most relaxing bath ever, I stood on the balcony with Marcus, sipping wine. I wore an elegant dress that hugged all my curves and dipped low enough on my chest to show the right amount of cleavage.

"Standing out here with you is incredibly peaceful and beautiful," I said, commenting about the view below. "It has always been one of my favorite places in the castle."

"I know," Marcus said.

I smiled. There was only one way I could see this evening getting better, and that was if the other two men were here. "What are Bret and Jax up to?"

"They are out on assignment," he said. "Why?"

I shrugged. "Just curious."

I wasn't the only one dressed sharply. Marcus had on a well-tailored suit, matching the color of my dress. Navy blue. I kept staring at him, wondering why I had never seen him dressed so nicely before. It was a gorgeous sight and I wanted to see more nights like this one happen.

"So, are you ready to tell me what this is all about yet?" I asked.

"You really don't do well with surprises," he said and shook his head while laughing under his breath.

"I do just fine with surprises, thank you very much," I said.

Someone behind us cleared their throat. I turned and settled my gaze on Bret. He smirked. And holy hell, he was dressed up as well. Though his suit was tailored in a different cut, everything else was the same.

"You're in this too?" I asked.

He tugged on his jacket and posed. "Pretty sharp, huh?"

"I'll say," I said and walked toward him.

"Dinner is served," he said to Marcus then bobbed his eyebrows at me.

I laughed as he held out his arm to lead me. I took it and we walked toward the kitchen together. I was almost worried about where we were going because I expected the lights to be on, but when we turned the corner, the glow of candlelight filled the room.

I gasped at the arrangement centered on the island.

Jax stood off to the side, dressed the same as the other two. He smiled as I met his gaze.

"This is so beautiful," I said.

Marcus walked up behind me, placing his hand on the small of my back. He leaned in and whispered, "Surprise!"

I giggled. "Thank you very much."

Bret pulled out a seat for me and I slid onto the chair, setting my wine glass on the island next to my plate setting.

"You guys have outdone yourselves," I said.

"Or maybe we haven't done enough yet," Jax said.

"What does that mean?" I asked, staring at him basked in the light from the candles.

He shrugged. "Exactly what I said."

I narrowed my gaze on him before settling it on the other two. "I have a feeling there is more you're not telling me."

"Just put some food on your plate already, woman," Bret said as he and Marcus took a seat.

I gave in, for the moment, and piled my plate with prime rib, Caesar salad, roasted potatoes, corn on the cob, and a dinner roll. Once the men started to dish themselves up, I dug in.

About halfway through the meal, we were deep into laughter. Once we settled down, I heard a strange sound coming from one of the men and looked up in time to catch Jax nodding at Marcus. He cleared his throat and took my hand, pulling my attention to him.

Why did the small, innocent action make my heart skip a beat? I wasn't for sure, but something told me that this was the other part of the surprise. I gulped and stared into Marcus's eyes.

"Today, we are celebrating someone wonderful, powerful, graceful, and beautiful," he said.

I smiled.

Jax added, "This person is feisty in all the best and worst ways, knows what she wants, and doesn't let anyone stop her from following her heart."

Bret brushed the back of his fingers along my arm. "This person is one in a million, who has shown incredible strength, courage, and love."

I giggled, though there were tears that stabbed at my eyes. "You guys are celebrating me?"

A collection of affirmations came from them.

"Awe… you all are so sweet," I said. "But why?"

"For starters," Jax said. "You helped save my life."

"And your quick thinking on the battlefield also saved mine," Marcus said.

"You are a force to reckon with," Bret added. "One who shouldn't be second-guessed or underestimated."

"You handled yourself in ways we never thought could be possible," Marcus finished.

"I surprised myself as well. I guess the thought of you guys getting hurt really had me digging deep into skills and powers I didn't even know I had," I said.

Each of the men held up their wine glasses. I followed suit.

In unison, they said, "To Emily."

Bret added, "The biggest badass around."

I laughed and then took a sip of the wine. "Thank you so much. You all certainly know how to make a girl feel truly special."

"Good, because we want to ask you something," Marcus said.

"I'm listening," I replied.

"We know that you had the intention of only staying here temporarily," he started, "But we were hoping you would consider staying longer."

"How much longer?" I asked.

Jax said, "How about forever?"

I blushed. "I don't know."

"Before you answer, I think it's important for you to know that what these two hardheads haven't said is we want you to be our woman. Stay with us. Be with us," Bret added.

"Like date the three of you at the same time?" I asked.

"Isn't that what we've been doing this entire time?" Marcus asked.

I shrugged, unsure if that was what we were doing or not. I never looked close enough to make that determination. "I guess I never saw it that way."

"So, what will it be?" Bret asked.

"I have to think about it," I said.

"What's there to think about?" Jax asked. "The four of us make perfect sense."

I pointed to Marcus. "Didn't you say you refused to share me?"

"Let's say that circumstances had changed for me, and leave it at that, okay?" He took another sip of his wine.

I sat back and thought about how the men made sense. We did make a perfect team. And I sort of already considered them my men. And the idea of living without them caused an ache in my chest that made it hard to breathe.

When I think of my future, it's with them. All of them. I couldn't think of a life where they weren't in it. They were a part of me. A part of my heart. And though I wasn't sure how we would work out the details of a relationship with the four of us, the idea felt right.

My heart skipped a beat. Excitement bubbled through me.

"We do make a great team," I said through a smile.

"Is that a yes?" Jax asked.

I nodded.

"Then let's make this thing official and consummate!" Bret stood from the island and swooped me up, tossing me over his shoulders. Marcus and Jax followed behind. Once we made it to my room, Bret tossed me on the bed and smiled at me.

I giggled. These men were too much.

They each did a striptease, removing their clothes and gazing at me with so much need in their eyes I instantly became aroused. Then they took turns taking off my clothes. And once I was naked, I moved to the center of the bed. My three men surrounded me, touching me in places and in ways that were highly erotic.

I sank into the mattress and sighed.

This was a perfect end to a perfect day. And I looked forward to many, many more like this.

EPILOGUE: SILAS

I sat in my chair behind my desk, staring out the picture window which overlooked downtown Boston. Drops of rain trickled down the glass, reflecting tiny, upside-down reflections of the city. The sight used to thrill me. I would find wonder in all the things that I had taken for granted as a human. But my wonder seemed to have worn out years ago. It took a lot to pique my interest anymore.

To say the least, I was full of melancholy. Every year was the same. Nothing seemed to change. There was nothing new.

The door to my office opened. Footsteps paddled in. I smelled the human before I heard his heartbeat. Which was unusual for me. But my mind had been rather preoccupied as of late.

"Excuse me, sir," my butler said. He was an older gentleman and had been in my employ for as long as I could remember.

I dragged my gaze to him. "Yes, Michael?"

"You have a visitor," he said, he lowered his head out of respect.

I waved the servant off. "I'm not taking visitors today. Tell him whatever it is he's selling I'm not interested in. Do whatever it is you need to. Just make him go away."

"I understand, sir," Michael said. "But the man insists on meeting with you immediately. Naturally, I already tried to scare him off. He was unmoved."

I quirked an eyebrow. "Interesting. Does he know who I am?"

The butler nodded. "Yes, sir."

I sat back in my chair and considered the new development as something I probably needed to pay closer attention to. The sudden visitor certainly broke through the monotony. Perhaps, the human would provide some level of entertainment before he became lunch.

"Very well," I said. "Send the man with the death wish in."

The butler nodded. "Right away, sir."

I sat straighter in my chair and watched as the butler left, leaving the door open. I listened to the rhythm of the man's heart as he stepped closer to my door. Interestingly enough, the beats of his heart remained even. That was odd considering humans had an innate response in their nervous systems when predators came too close. This man seemed immune to such things.

Entertaining, indeed.

A tall man with long, curly hair, and a thin beard covering his face stepped in. He carried himself in a way that gave the impression he was used to being in charge and having his commands being met. Maybe he thought of us as equals, though the thought made me want to laugh.

Not even in a thousand years would he ever come close to being my equal. But I figured if he had the courage to walk into the proverbial lion's den, I could spare a few minutes of my time hearing him out.

Needless to say, I was becoming more and more curious about this man.

He walked to the front of my desk and nodded.

I smirked. "You've done your research."

"I pride myself on knowing who I intend to do business with," he said.

"And who are you?" I asked.

"Collin Morris," he said.

I nodded. "Well, Collin Morris, what business did you intend to strike with me?"

"I want your help in ridding myself of some people who have done me wrong," he said.

I snorted. "Is that all?"

He shook his head. "I want you to fight with me. An army of vampires against shifters."

"Who was it to have wronged you so terribly that you would knowingly walk into a vampire's home and ask for help without a single thought as to your own safety."

He leveled his gaze on me. "As I said, I pride myself in knowing about who I intend to do business with."

"Yes. I suppose you had mentioned as much," I said and returned my attention to the picture window. "What would be my compensation for aiding you in your quest? And before you answer, I want you to know that it had better be worth my time to not only break a peace treaty which has been in place for hundreds of years but worth the war it would unleash."

His gaze hardened. I almost laughed. He said, "You get to keep what you kill."

"Intriguing offer, but I'm going to pass. I'm not convinced it would be worth my time. Thank you for the offer. You may leave," I said and turned my attention toward my window again. The little interaction with the human wasn't entertaining for as long as I had hoped. His entertainment proved disappointing, and I was becoming bored.

The man huffed. "I demand that I have retribution for the wrongs done to me. You must help me."

"Or what?" I asked, settling my gaze on him.

The man stammered. I smiled, flashing my fangs. He gulped. His heart raced a few ticks faster. The reaction renewed my interest in the man.

Calmly, I said, "If you feel so strongly about your quest, you should figure it out on your own, or ask someone else willing to help. You are not worth the war."

"That didn't work out for me in the past," he said. "You are my last option."

I rolled my eyes, having grown bored of him. "As I said, pass. See yourself out."

When the man didn't move, I stared him deep in the eyes. "Or did you want to be lunch?"

He shook his head, huffed a few times, and then stormed out of the room. I smirked to myself as the door slammed closed. The shadows within the room shifted and moved forward. Xavier, my head guard, and Brock, my son, stepped forward.

"Let me guess, you want me to actually give some thought to his offer?" I asked.

Brock said, "Well, of course, I think we should do it. We're the most powerful creatures in all the realms combined."

"You are still young and have much to learn about the ways of the world, my son," I said.

"I'm three-hundred and fifty years old. I know enough," he said.

I looked at Xavier. He shrugged. "There is more to the man's request than what he had said. My suggestion is to figure out what that is before making a final decision."

I leaned back and fell into my thoughts. What good would a war with the humans do for us? We had plenty of food. Even slaves that provided for us when we needed. I was bored, granted, but not enough to stir a pot of chaos. However, what Xavier said made sense. There was much more than what was being said. Perhaps, I had dismissed the human too quickly.

"Very well," I said then settled my attention Xavier. "Find out what you can and report back to me."

He nodded and instantly left.

Brock glared at me and shook his head. "When did you become so soft?"

"To what are you referring to?" I asked.

"In another time, you would have drained the human just for walking into a place he didn't belong in. Yet you not only let him leave, but you sent Xavier to spy on him. What gives?"

I sighed. "It isn't a matter of being soft, my son. Not every human needs to die because they crossed my path. Besides, this is a tactful way of handling an issue. If he becomes a problem, then I would gladly drain him, as you so elegantly put it."

Brock shook his head. "I still think you've gone soft."

I narrowed my eyes on him. I knew exactly what my son wanted. And I had little reason not to give it to him. I had suspected for a time that he was growing restless and sought out his own means of entertainment. , was why I turned a blind eye to his so-called secret activities. But perhaps, he could be of use to me when it came to the human.

I sighed. "So be it. Capture the human and hold him in the cells below the estate. Make him talk, but don't kill him. If you can drag out of him a solid reason to go to war, I will give that to you. Otherwise, my final decision will stand."

Brock smiled. "With pleasure."

He turned and started to walk away. Before he could disappear, I added, "I meant what I said. If you kill him, you won't get what you want."

He glanced at me from over his shoulder and without another word left me to my solitude.

My attention fell once again on the picture window. It appeared as though things were changing after all.

Loved Red and Her Dragons? Continue reading Silas' story **here** in the next book in this series.

Three gorgeous as gods vampires want to worship me as their own.
Too hot to handle.
Wild, enigmatic, and mind-blowing… and the things they can do to me.
But then there is also one human man…

What had started out as a joke—a means for revenge—turned into me sneaking through a mansion that was thought to be abandoned.

A mansion occupied by three startlingly gorgeous vampires who could be gods.

Grab your copy here in Kindle Unlimited.

BEAUTY AND HER BEASTS
(SNEAK PEEK)

DESCRIPTION

I did what no woman was supposed to do.

I fought my way through college, landed a job at a hotel far, far away
from my dead-end town.
A job in a *man's* position.
And I seemed to be immensely attracted to the gardener, the cook,
and the owner of the hotel.

I'm forever aroused by my three, hot men, and they know it.
They don't stick around to do anything about it, though.
I might just spontaneously combust.

And then, there's my controlling ex-boyfriend.
He reared his ugly head, demanding my release.
I'm forced to put my foot down to save my men from literal torches
and pitch forks.

No one is going to tell me what to do, much less who to love.
Mess with me if you dare.
My three hot, shifter men would be the less of your worries.

PROLOGUE

Wendell Pierce, Allana's father, sat at the quaint kitchen table in the nook of their cottage. He slowly sipped on a hot cup of coffee while Allana pursued the wanted section of the local paper of a nearby town. It was her last break in college, and she wanted to get a head start on getting a job before she graduated. The last thing she wanted was to spend the rest of her days in a boorish town like *Fleuve Ville*.

Not that she regretted growing up in the town. It was only a dead-end for her. A means to an end. The only thing this town had to offer her was the home she grew up in and her papa. That was all, and she wanted so much more for herself. To see the world and live life on her terms. The consequences be damned.

Besides, all she had ever known from the people of this river town was hatred for being different. People even cast a side-eye at her father for tolerating her going to college in the first place. But Allana was as smart as she was beautiful. She might not have been stick-figure thin like most of the girls in town, and that was just fine by her. It was the words the people used that turned her off from giving the town another second of her time. She heard it all growing up. The nasty comments about her weight and never being able to get a man.

"Would it be so bad to work a couple of years here before setting off to another town?" Wendell asked his daughter as he focused on the name of the paper. The Sentinel was in large bold font heading the top of the paper. It laid on the table between the two of them, cast aside by Allana in favor of the classifieds.

Allana shrugged. "I would much rather not work here, Papa. Besides, I'll come to visit you often."

"What about that man you were seeing? What was his name?" Wendell stared out of the window as though the answer waited for him right outside the pane of glass.

"Collin?" Allana offered. "He's long gone and for good reason."

She shifted uncomfortably, cleared her throat, and then refocused on the paper in front of her. The topic of the man she used to date was a sore subject and she would rather not spend another moment thinking about him. If she ever saw him again, it would be too soon.

"You remember what I told you a few years ago?" he asked. "About marriage."

When Allana was twenty-five years old and just heading off to college—it had taken her years to get accepted, thanks to the masochistic society they live in—her father had sat her down and suggested that she might be safer in the world with a man by her side. The town might be used to her confident ways, but other towns might not be so accepting or accommodating without her being married. He hated telling her such things, knowing his daughter preferred to carve her own way through the world, but he knew it was "just the way of things."

She had told him she would change "the way of things," and so far, she was doing exactly that. Making her mark on the world and leaving behind a legacy for the Pierce name. Already she had proven herself to be quite the scholar and landed herself in the good graces of a couple Professors. She, despite her gender, was top of her class.

Allana shifted her gaze upward to meet her father's eyes. "Yeah. I remember."

There was hesitation in her voice. She knew her father wouldn't press the issue, but perhaps there was a good reason for him bringing it up again after so long.

He smiled at her, eyes crinkling at the corners. His brown eyes sparkling in the soft morning light. "I was proud of you then. I'm proud of you now. I have been, and will always be, proud of you."

Allana smiled. "Thank you, Papa."

She sighed and slammed the paper down on the table. "I'm done with this for now."

"No luck?" he asked.

She shook her head. "But I'm not giving up."

"The right job will come along. You'll see," Wendell said. "It will happen when you least expect it."

Allana settled her gaze on her father. She stepped up to him and kissed him on the cheek. "I know, Papa. But it's not like it's simply going to fall into my lap."

Wendell let out a deep chuckle. "With you, anything is possible."

* * *

THE DEATH of Jacinda and Phillip Heller was sudden and heartbreaking. Even more so for King who had been distant ever since he came back from the war, down an arm. Gunnar had done his best to keep his sadness at bay for the sake of his job. He was the cook and had been for years. It was his job to feed all the people who showed up for the wake following the funeral. Everyone depended on him, and he hated the idea of letting anyone down.

While he worked in the kitchen, cleaning up from the feast he had made for all those who came to pay their respects, he caught sight of King rushing past the doorway to the kitchen, likely on his way into the bowels of the castle turned hotel. Gunnar ran after him knowing if he didn't catch him now, King would disappear for another few weeks, if not longer. Gunnar never could figure out where the man slept, much less why he would choose such a desolate place to live, and so long as King was standoffish, that would remain so.

"King," Gunnar shouted.

He didn't respond. If anything, King picked up the pace to try and get out of the confrontation. Though he never seemed to hate

Gunnar, he did give the impression he merely tolerated him. Gunnar wasn't going to give up so easily. He picked up his pace as well, reaching the corner King had turned at seconds before.

"I have to talk to you," Gunnar said.

King growled as he halted. He didn't turn around to face the cook, instead kept his back toward the man. "What?"

Gunnar held up his hands as he approached, despite King not seeing his gesture. "I only wanted to check in on you. You've been more broody than usual."

"Happens when your parents are killed," King said and started to walk again.

"Look, I know it's no consolation, but I'm sorry. I loved them too. Now that you are the head of the business, I have some important things to address with you."

"Can it wait?" King asked.

"Normally yes, but—" Gunnar started.

"Then wait." King continued down the long corridor and disappeared into a break in the wall.

Gunnar stared after the guy, frustrated. He couldn't really blame King for his deteriorating mood. The maids who had worked here since King was a child told Gunnar stories about how charming and outgoing King was before the war. Guess the guy had demons he was fighting here at home too. Nightmares that wouldn't let him go. And now with the tragic loss of his parents, it would be even more time before King brightened up again.

If that ever happened.

What King needed was a reason to live.

The thought sparked an idea in Gunnar's mind. He turned his tail around and went to find Declan who was likely outside on the grounds, finishing up his duties for the day.

Declan was a loner in a sense. He and King had never gotten along. Or so Gunnar had been told. He hadn't seen much interaction between the two of them, what with King being ever reclusive. Gunnar didn't mind Declan. Especially for a half-breed. He kept to himself, got his job done, and didn't start problems. To Gunnar, Declan was an all-right kind of guy.

Gunnar immediately found Declan at the tool shed near the ground's border. Declan nodded in greeting as he heard Gunnar coming from miles away. Gunnar wasn't trying to sneak up on the guy. He made his approach detectable on purpose.

"What can I do for you, Gunnar?" he asked. His dirty blond hair was pulled back low, tied at the nape of his neck. His beard dripped with sweat from his hard work.

"We need to talk," Gunnar said. "About King."

Declan sighed and faced Gunnar, eying him with his icy blues. "What has he done now?"

"It's what he's not doing that I'm concerned about," Gunnar said.

Declan locked up the shed then turned and leaned against the outside wall. "You are aware that we have no love lost between us, right?"

"I've been told, but hear me out," Gunnar said. "This business is going to tank within the next few months if we don't get something working. Now, I know we don't hang out often and I don't know you incredibly well, but I know enough to make the assumption that losing this job isn't something you want. I think King needs a thing to live for. Something to look forward to. And I have a way I think we could achieve that."

Declan snorted as he folded his massive arms in front of him. "Good luck with that."

"I'm serious. We have to hire a manager, for starters. The hotel has been in the red for the last few months, and the funeral was not cheap. But we need someone else to be the face of the hotel. Someone gorgeous and who will get King's attention."

"Playing matchmaker? You really think a woman will get King out of his hole?" Declan asked.

Gunnar shrugged. "Something has to happen or we're both going to be out of a job soon."

"I seriously doubt a girl will work," Declan said. "No matter how beautiful. You're better off hiring a woman of the night and be done with it. As far as the manager, I'll make some flyers. You can hand them out the next time you head out to market."

Gunnar sighed. It wasn't what he was hoping for, but it wasn't the worst-case scenario. Declan could have laughed him off. Still, he had hoped for a little more than what he got. "All right. Fine. But I have a gut feeling you'll eat your words."

Declan copped a crooked smile. "We'll see, my friend."

Gunnar said his farewell and headed to his room to plan. If he was going to find a woman worthy of King, he was going to have to go farther out than he normally would. A woman like that would be increasingly hard to find. Gunnar knew of the women in the towns he frequented for supplies and none of them came close to the one he was searching for. Going farther was the only option.

Once in his room, he pulled out a map of the country and circled several locations surrounding the *Chateau*. One of them was the town of *Fleuveville*. His eyes stared at the town and wondered why he felt pulled to go there. It lay outside of the *Dusang* forest. He had never been there before, but he was called to go, like a magnet. Now he just needed to find the time to go there and a good excuse.

Continue reading this sizzling hot and dirty reverse harem romance here in Kindle Unlimited.

GET THE ENTIRE DIRTY PARANORMAL FAIRYTALE HAREMLAND SERIES HERE

All books in the Dirty Paranormal Fairytale Haremland series are steamy, standalone, reverse harem shifter romances with an HEA and FREE to read in Kindle Unlimited.

Book 1: Beauty and Her Beasts

Book 2: Alice and Her Shifters

Book 3: Goldie and Her Bears

Book 4: Read and Her Dragons

Book 5: Cinderella and Her Vampires

LISA'S INSIDER CLUB

Join my insider group for fan exclusives, new release information and occasional freebies. I promise I'll NEVER spam you.